The
Same Place
but Different

The
Same Place
but Different

◆

Perry Nodelman

Simon & Schuster Books for Young Readers

Simon & Schuster Books for Young Readers
An imprint of Simon & Schuster Children's Publishing Division
1230 Avenue of the Americas
New York, NY 10020
Copyright © 1995 by Perry Nodelman
Simon & Schuster Books for Young Readers is a
trademark of Simon & Schuster.
Designed by David Neuhaus
The text of this book is set in Janson Text 11.5 pts.
Manufactured in the United States of America
10 9 8 7 6 5 4 3 2 1
Library of Congress Cataloging-in-Publication Data
Nodelman, Perry. The same place but different / Perry Nodelman. p. cm.
Summary: Young John Nesbit enters the world of the Strangers in order to
rescue his baby sister, whom the fairies have replaced with a Changeling.
ISBN 0-671-89839-6 [1. Fairies—Fiction. 2. Fantasy.] I. Title.
PZ7.N67175Sam 1995 [Fic]—dc20 94-13064 CIP AC

To Mrs. Isaac

The
Same Place
but Different

One

The hill opened, and my life changed.

It happened on a Thursday afternoon after school. There was the usual mindless junk on TV, my homework was too boring to even think about, and my buddies Mark and Rob were at hockey practice. It was winter, see, and they were *always* at hockey practice. So I didn't have anything to do, and I didn't want to do anything anyway.

Besides, my mother was nagging at me. I should get out more often, she said. I am only going to be young once and I should enjoy it while I can. I should get out my skates and go over to the rink at the community club and get some exercise.

Exercise. Ha. What she meant was hockey. A

bunch of muscle-brained hulks getting their jollies from committing life-threatening acts of violence, otherwise known as bodychecking.

"I hate hockey," I said. "I will *not* play hockey, and that's that."

Mom gave me the look she always gives me when we have this conversation. Sort of like the queen of England watching a skunk spray one of her corgies.

I gave the look right back to her, just like I always do. And finally she turned away, just like she always does.

But she always has the last word. "You mark me, Johnny Nesbit," she said from over her shoulder. "Someday that willfulness of yours is going to get you into a lot of trouble."

Don't get me wrong. I love my mom. But ever since this thing happened to the baby, she just seemed to be at me all the time. I knew she didn't really mean it, that it was just because of what had happened to Andrea. But it was getting on my nerves. I decided to go out.

I put on my ski jacket, and we went through all the usual don't-forget-your-mittens-and-put-on-your-hat-and-don't-be-late-for-dinner stuff. I said, "Yeah, Mom, sure" enough times to make her happy, and then I went out and closed the door.

And stood there on the back step. I didn't know what to do or where to go.

No way was I going to the community club, where I would have to watch my so-called friends blissfully bodycheck each other into pulp. I could have used a sugar hit, but I didn't have any cash, so there wasn't any point in heading up to the 7-Eleven.

Anyway, the last thing I needed was to wade my way through that bunch of turkeys from my school who are always hanging out there by Sev, nattering on about the excellent drugs they're supposedly doing and the excellent babes they're supposedly making it with. Yeah, sure, and I'm the reincarnation of Elvis.

No, what I wanted to do was just get away, from everybody and everything. I was mad at my mom. I was mad at my useless hockey-playing friends. And I guess I was mad at my baby sister, Andrea, who just sat there in her crib all the time and never blinked and never said a word and never did anything but poop in her diapers. I just didn't want to be with other people for a while.

Well, the only place I know within walking distance of my house that doesn't feel like people is the Monkey Paths down in the park. So I decided to go there.

The park is really just a floodplain—a long flat strip between Churchill Drive and the river, a place to hold water if the river overflows in the spring. There's hardly even any trees there, except for a few lined up along the river. But there is one bigger patch of trees, old high ones, right near the bridge that goes over the river into St. Vital. It's hilly where those trees are, and there are trails going up and down the hills where people fool around on their bikes. That's the Monkey Paths.

It's a different kind of place, the Monkey Paths. It doesn't feel like people down there. I don't know why, because even if you're standing right in the middle of the trees you can still see the houses over on the other side of the river, and you can always hear the cars on the bridge. Plus which, at any moment you could get run down by some showboater going too fast on cross-country skis.

But it still feels different. Uncivilized, sort of. That's why I decided to go there. I was feeling uncivilized myself.

The Monkey Paths were disappointing. In the summer at least there are leaves on the trees, and you can pretend the city is far away. In the winter it's just bare trunks and ski trails and dog poop everywhere you look, showing up nicely in contrast to the snow. And it was rush hour already, and all those cars on the bridge were making a huge roar.

Worst of all, there was some guy screaming at a little kid over by the swings at the top of the hill. The kid was bawling because she wanted a swing. I mean, it was the middle of February, right? The swings were buried up to their seats in snow. You'd think the guy would have figured that out *before* he wasted all that time bundling the poor kid into the snowsuit and the scarves and the mittens and the boots.

Finally the guy just threw the kid onto his toboggan and dragged her off, she bawling all the way and he screaming at her to shut up. And me thinking, boy, if it was Andrea doing that bawling, we sure wouldn't be screaming at her, we'd be shouting for joy.

Then for a moment, at least, I was alone—as alone as I was going to be. No people. No noise except the dull roar of the cars, and some dogs barking off in the distance. So I sat down. In the snow. With my back to the bridge and the river and the houses over on the other side.

I didn't have anything better to do.

So I'm sitting there, so busy thinking about how miserable my life is that I'm not really paying much attention to anything. Not that there was much of anything to pay attention to. All I could see was the side of a hill with some bare bushes growing out of it. I sat there just sort of not looking at the side of that hill.

Then, I blinked. I blinked because—well, this is hard to describe—but the hill didn't seem to be there anymore. At least, it was there, but there seemed to be a hole in it or something. Almost like a window, except it didn't have any glass.

There I am looking at some bushes with snow on them, and all at once there's this window. Jeez. I nearly jumped out of my ski jacket.

I blinked and then looked again. The hole was still there. I looked closer.

Through the hole, the inside of the hill looked hollow. Like a room. And there was a woman in the room. She was wearing a long dress, sort of a nightgown, and she was sitting there in this weird-looking old chair with carving all over it. And she was nursing a baby.

Well.

I was just about to move my butt out of there, before a vampire came along and sucked my blood or something, when the woman looked up from the baby and noticed me.

"John!" she said. "John Nesbit! It is you, isn't it, Johnny?"

That did it. I mean, this woman sits calmly inside a hill—*inside*, mind you—not three blocks from my own perfectly ordinary house over on good old ordinary Wavell Avenue, where at this very moment my more or less ordinary mother is using all the wonders of modern science to prepare my perfectly ordinary preformed, preshaped, and prepackaged modern dinner. And this woman inside a hill knows my name.

This was obviously not your usual visit to the park.

"It *is* Johnny?" she said again, and it began to dawn on me that I wasn't really being very bothered by all of this. I mean, I knew I wasn't dreaming or anything. I was wide awake and I was talking to a person inside a hill. I should have been jumping out of my skin, but the way she said my name sounded sort of familiar. So I looked at her more closely. She *was* sort of familiar.

"Mrs. Fordyce?" I said.

"It *is* you," she said. "It *is* Johnny Nesbit."

And it *was* Mrs. Fordyce, too. Which was pretty weird. Because you see, Mrs. F. died last summer. I was talking to a dead person.

Two

Mrs. F. was sort of a buddy of mine, before she died. She lived just a few houses down from us, and I got to know her last year when I was delivering papers. She never treated me like a dumb kid the way most of them do. She never yelled at me about walking on her precious lawn, and she never carried on about what lazy good-for-nothings kids are today, just because her paper happened to be a few minutes late. And she never giggled and told me how a nice-looking boy like me must have my pick of the girls.

Mrs. F. never said stuff like that. I felt bad when she died.

She was having a baby and she just died all of a sudden, there in the hospital. Even the doctor was shocked, at least according to my mom. I could remember her talking about how they didn't know there was anything wrong with Mrs. F. She wasn't even sick.

And now she was sitting inside the hill on that weird chair and talking to me.

"I...I thought you were dead," I said. Clever, eh? Well, what *would* you say? Considering the circumstances, it was better than "Nice weather we're having."

"I wish I *was* dead," she said, giving me this mournful look. "I wish I was."

"But what happened? What are you—?" I was so confused that I didn't even know what to ask.

"I'm not sure I know what happened myself. I was lying there in St. Boniface Hospital, having contractions. Labor pains, you know? They were getting closer and closer and it hurt, it really hurt bad. The nurses told me it wouldn't hurt, but it did, and I remember how mad I was about being lied to. Maybe it happened because I was mad. Maybe *they* thought I'd called to them or something. Anyway, all of a sudden it didn't hurt anymore. And I wasn't in the hospital. I was here. Here in the castle."

"The castle?" I was confused. "But you're in the park; you're at the Monkey Paths."

"No, Johnny, I'm not. I wish I were, but I'm not. *They* stole me away. *Stole* me!"

She stopped and shivered. I didn't know what she meant, but whatever it was, it scared her.

It scared me, too. I changed the subject.

"But this is stupid, Mrs. F.," I said. "I'm here and you're here, so we don't have to worry about it anymore, right? I mean, you just come out through that window and come home with me. I'll lend you my jacket. It's not that cold out today anyway, and it's only a few blocks, and you can—"

"I can't, Johnny, I can't leave," she said. "It's not possible—not anymore. I'm here *forever!*"

Why wasn't it possible? And where did she think she was?

"Where are you?" I said. I moved closer to the window, trying to see the room she sat in.

"Here in the land of the . . . of the . . ." For some reason she didn't want to say what came next. "Well, sometimes they're called Strangers."

"Strangers?" This didn't make any sense to me at all. *What* strangers? Aliens from another planet? Immigrants from Hong Kong? The bad people adults are always telling little kids they're not supposed to talk to?

"Yes," she went on, "sometimes they're called Strangers. But their real name used to scare people to death, and it should still, believe me, Johnny. They are—" She paused. "The fairies."

Fairies???

That's right, that's what she said. Fairies. Those cute little guys with wings we used to read about in grade two. Or else it's just another word like "fag" or "queer"—one of the names those turkeys in front of Sev like to call gay guys, in case people don't realize just from looking at their ugly sneering faces how macho they are themselves.

Mrs. F. got stuck inside a hill by fairies???

"I know, I know," she said. "It sounds crazy. But they do exist, Johnny. They're real, and they've captured me. You've got to warn other people before it's too late!"

Well, it isn't every day that you talk to a dead friend inside a hill who tells you that a bunch of little guys with wings and magic wands are plotting to take over the world. So maybe, I told myself, Mrs. F. didn't die in the hospital after all. Maybe she just had a breakdown or something, and they hushed it up. Yeah, and her husband kept her locked up in the house because he didn't want anyone to know what happened to her. And now she'd escaped from the house and that was why she was in the park.

That was it. That had to be it. And I had to get her back home before she froze to death in that skimpy nightgown thing she was wearing.

I started to climb up the hill and lift myself up through the hole.

I couldn't.

It wasn't there. There wasn't any hole to climb into.

I mean, there had to be. It looked like a hole. But when I reached out for it, all I felt was the snow on the side of the hill. There I was talking to Mrs. F., and I could see her clearly, but I couldn't get in. Mrs. F. was inside, somehow, and I was outside. We were in the same place, but we weren't in the same place.

So maybe she wasn't crazy. Maybe I was the crazy one. I sat down again.

"Johnny, please, I know it's hard to believe, but please try. I'm not where you are, in the park. I'm here with the Strangers. Here forever. I don't know how long they're going to let me see you, or even if they know it's happening. They're so unpredictable."

She was getting excited again. "That's why it's so important, Johnny. That's why you have to do something, tell somebody. The police, the army, I don't know. Maybe the Anglican bishop." She giggled in a crazy way. "Yes, they came from England, didn't they? Maybe the Anglican bishop is the one to tell."

It scared me, that giggle. I mean, it really scared me. I was just about ready to take off. But then she shook herself a little and looked like her old self again.

"I'm sorry, Johnny," she said. "Please don't be scared. You've got to do something, let people know about it so it doesn't happen to anybody else. Tell them I've been captured by the Strangers. They've found a way into our country, and if someone doesn't stop them, they'll—" She got this terrified look on her face. "No, it's too horrible. Somebody has to stop them."

"Don't worry," I said, trying to reassure her. She was getting too excited, and I didn't want to hear that giggling again. "I'll tell them."

"And watch out for Strangers, Johnny," she added, her voice more urgent. "Some of them are dangerous. Watch out for them. You can tell them by their nostrils."

"Their nostrils?"

"Yes. They have only one."

"One—?" One nostril? Only one hole in the bottom of their noses? This was getting weirder by the minute. "But—"

"No more questions. Time is running out. I can sense it, I—Just tell people. And, Johnny?"

"Yes?"

"This baby I'm holding. You know it's not mine, don't you, Johnny?"

It wasn't?

"They brought me here so I could nurse this baby instead of my own—my own baby, the one I looked forward to, the one I—" She almost cried, but then she got hold of herself again. "And I *have* nursed her, I have! She's never had anything but breast milk, not ever! That's why *you* have to do something. For yourself. For your mom. Soon."

For me? For Mom? What was she talking about?

"Look, Johnny," she said urgently, holding the baby out toward me. "Look at the baby."

I looked at it. I looked at it real good. And I didn't have anything to say.

Because I knew that baby.

It was Andrea. My sister. My baby sister who sat in her crib and did nothing but stare all day. It was Andrea, and she was reaching toward me and smiling.

"But she's at home," I said. "In her crib, she's—"

"That's not Andrea, Johnny. *This* is Andrea. That . . . that thing you have at home isn't Andrea. It's one of them, it's a Ch—"

Shazzam. She didn't even get to finish her sentence. All of a sudden she wasn't there.

Mrs. F. wasn't there, and Andrea wasn't there, and the hole in the hill wasn't there either.

Cars were zooming by on the bridge. There were ski trails and dog poop everywhere. And I was sitting with my nose pressed into the side of a hill, looking at nothing but snow.

Three

I walked home slowly, not paying much attention to the barking I kept hearing off in the distance. Just thinking about it all.

Thinking especially about Andrea.

I mean, sure, Mrs. F. was a good guy and I liked her, but she was just someone I delivered papers to. I was sorry about her but it didn't really bother me all that much. But Andrea—Andrea was my sister. And if that was Andrea inside that hill, then it was something else lying in the crib at home.

Something that wasn't human.

To tell the truth, I kind of suspected it wasn't human even before Mrs. F. told me. Oh, I know you're supposed to love your sister and all that. But Andrea wasn't easy to love.

It wasn't just that she sat there in her crib all the time and never did anything. What really got me was what she was doing to my folks.

My mom and dad used to be okay before she came. We used to have some good times.

And don't think I was jealous. I know all about sibling rivalry and I didn't have it. By the time Andrea was born I was already way too old for that. I hardly needed anybody to change my dydees and read me bedtime stories anymore.

And besides which, before this thing happened to her, I liked having Andrea. I liked holding her. I even kind of liked changing her diapers. It was fun, in a gross sort of way.

Yeah, we were all happy back then. My mom had somebody else to fuss about instead of me. Even *I* had somebody to fuss about instead of me. Everything was fine.

Then Andrea stopped smiling. All of a sudden. I mean, she was coming along nicely, crying so loud in the middle of the night that she even woke *me* up sometimes. And she was crawling around and getting into everything and generally being a nuisance. She was just your ordinary everyday typical baby sister—and then one day, she wasn't. She stopped singing and crawling. Just stopped. From that day on she did nothing—nothing but stare and eat and poop.

And everything changed.

My folks would hardly ever talk to me anymore, or to each other. Oh, sure, Mom shouted a lot, but neither of them *talked*. They spent the whole time worrying about Andrea, and taking Andrea to doctors, and having Andrea tested, and finding out that the doctors were deeply deeply sorry, but no, they couldn't do anything about Andrea. Mom shouted at Dad, and Dad sat there listening to Mom shout at him and sighed a lot. Finally she stopped shouting, and they both just sighed a lot.

It's a good thing I was an emotionally mature human being already, because I sure wasn't getting much loving attention from those two. We were not a happy family.

The interesting thing was, it had all started last summer. Right around when Mrs. F. died. I mean, almost exactly the same day. I never connected the two things before, but now, well, it sort of made sense.

At least, if it really was Mrs. F. inside that hill, and if it really was Andrea she was holding.

If it was, then—that *thing* in the crib wasn't Andrea after all. Maybe somebody could exorcize it or ghost-bust it or something, and we could be a happy family again.

Plus which, of course, I had to save the entire civilized world from an invasion of evil strangers. Fairies. Like Mrs. F. said.

Trying to save the world from fairies is not something that's likely to win you many friends.

Who would believe me? *I* didn't believe me.

It was crazy. I knew it was crazy. So how was I going to get anybody else to believe me?

This was going to take some thought. That's why I walked home slowly. The weird barking I kept hearing off in the distance was just the right background for that kind of thinking.

And I guess I got pretty caught up in my thoughts, because the first words I said to my mom as I walked into the kitchen were exactly what was on my mind.

"Mom," I said, reaching for a cookie, "do you believe in fairies?"

Mom didn't say anything. Just glanced up from her frying pan full of pork chops and gave me one of her queen of England looks. Finally she sighed and said, "Very funny. Ho-ho. Go and wash your hands for dinner." Then she sighed again and looked back down at the pork chops.

Just like I thought. It was not going to be easy getting anybody to believe me.

On my way to the bathroom I decided to look in on Andrea. She was sitting in her crib, staring at me. I stared back at her. She stared back at me. Like always.

Andrea never blinked. Usually it made me so uncomfortable that I stopped looking at her. But this time I was determined. According to Mrs. F., this thing in the crib wasn't Andrea. It sure looked like Andrea, but if it wasn't her, then there had to be some little detail, something I could notice about her, that was different.

So I kept on staring. I resisted blinking with all the will I had. And for a moment—

Well, it was just for a moment, and then it was Andrea again. But in that moment, something sort of, well, sort of shifted. Something looked different, and it wasn't a baby I was staring at.

It was an old man, maybe. Sort of like an old man. A hairy little old man looking at me as if he'd like to slice me in half and eat me for dinner.

One moment only, and then he was gone. And for the first time in months, I was glad to see Andrea again, blank stare and all. Anything was better than that repulsive little thing with all the hair and wrinkles and that hateful look. It was too scary to think about. It couldn't be real.

I got myself together, more or less. I went to the john, took a leak, washed my hands, and went into the kitchen for dinner, all the while saying to myself, "It can't be, it can't be, it can't be."

It was quiet at dinner. It was always quiet at our house, ever since Andrea had changed. Dad had just sort of disappeared. He never said anything anymore except "Pass the peas." And, Mom, well, she only opened her mouth if she wanted to do some complaining about me, and she even seemed to be doing that less and less often. I guess I should have been happy, but you know, I sometimes deliberately did things she would be sure to complain about, just so I could hear a human voice at the dinner table. Hearing about how lazy I was and how sloppy I was and how willful I was was better than that endless ugly silence.

But that night it was just silence. Pork chops, potatoes, peas, and silence.

The silence was killing me. It was letting me think about Mrs. F., and about Andrea. Finally I couldn't stand it anymore. It was on my mind and I had to say it.

"Listen," I said. They both stopped eating and gave me this startled look, surprised to hear a voice during dinner.

"It's just that—" I stopped. No way I could tell them about the hole in the hill. "Well," I continued, "somebody told me . . . I mean . . . I read somewhere . . . yeah, I read in a book that people used to believe in fairies, right? And . . . and the fairies would take away human children and leave something else in their place. And, well, I was thinking about . . ."

I stopped. I could already tell from the look on Mom's face that this wasn't going to work.

"Yes, John," she said very quietly. "Go on. You were thinking about . . . ?"

I had to say it. "I was thinking about . . . Andrea."

Dead silence. Mom glared at me, and suddenly the appearance of my dinner became very fascinating. I gave it all my attention.

Mom finally spoke. "Andrea. You were thinking about Andrea." She grabbed my arm and gave me this piercing look. The peas I'd been forking up went flying.

"Now you listen here, John Nesbit. You're old

enough to know better than to—" She stopped and shuddered, still clutching me. It hurt like hell, and I couldn't pull my arm away.

"Your sister is sick, John. Sick. And that's that. You have to accept it. We all have to accept it. *I* have to—"

Suddenly she sobbed and gave herself a shake, and the fingers she had been digging into my arm went limp. And she just stopped talking and stared off into space.

There was silence again. Dad looked at me. I waited, hoping he'd say something—do something. Finally he did. He sighed, and then he started to shovel in his potatoes.

Four

It's the next morning, and I'm lying in my bed. I wake up, and I'm in my room. I'm in my bed in my room, and the blankets are pulled up over my head.

So far, so good. I almost always pull the blankets up over my head when I'm sleeping. I almost always wake up this way.

But this morning something's different. I wake up and I can't move. I can't move because a huge dog is lying on top of me. It's panting in my ear. I can't see it, but I know it's there.

It's there and it's lying on me, and it's heavy, so heavy. I can't figure out how this dog got in my room, but I don't have much time to worry about it, because it's crushing me. I can't breathe at all. I'm gasping, gasping, I—

I wake up. It's the next morning, and I'm lying in my bed. I wake up, and the sheets are pulled up over my head.

And there's no dog.

Of course there's no dog. It was a dream. I heard a dog outside. Lately there's been a lot of dogs barking in the neighborhood, enough for people to comment about them. They're strays, people say. You never see them but you hear them barking a lot. So I heard the strays barking while I was asleep, and I made the rest up.

It was just a dream.

The next few days just sort of went by. Nothing much happened. I knew I had to do something, tell someone, but I didn't know who or what. As I'd so skillfully discovered, Mom and Dad were out of the question. And I had enough sense to know that saying anything at all about fairies to my bodychecking buds would be sort of like stepping onto an airport runway in the path of a Concorde.

For one wild moment I even considered consulting one of my teachers. Actually going up to Mr. Milton or maybe McAlpine and saying, "Could you help me, sir? I have to save the world from total destruction and I can't figure out where to begin."

Well, if you knew Milton or McAlpine, you'd understand how desperate I was.

Anyway, it was just that one wild moment, and then I came to my senses. I didn't tell anybody and I didn't do anything. I just slept, woke up and ate my breakfast, went to school, came home, ate my dinner, slept again, and tried not to think about it.

And thought about it, all the time.

And each time I left the house and walked to school, or left school and walked home, I could hear dogs barking.

I was hearing that barking all the time now—all day long, all evening long, even in my sleep. Howling, whining, yelping. It sounded like a whole pack of dogs, a big pack, and the strange thing was, it seemed to be coming from up in the sky. I could hear them, but I never did see them. It was getting on my nerves.

One morning on the way to school, I heard that noise from the sky louder than ever, and even though I knew it was ridiculous, I stopped and looked up.

What I saw, off in the distance, was what looked like a flock of geese. Well, it was a little odd for geese to be around at that time of the year, maybe. But winter was almost over, so they were really just a few weeks early. It had to be geese.

Not dogs but geese. Honking, not barking. Now that I was paying close attention to it, it didn't even sound all that much like barking.

Or so I told myself. And the days passed, and nothing unusual happened, and I decided that the best thing was to just forget about it and get on with my life. Maybe I would even take up hockey, just to keep my mind off other things, such as real life. It seemed to work for my numb-brain friends.

But first I decided to have just one more look at that hill. The one where I saw Mrs. F.

I don't know what I expected to find there. Nope, sorry, that's a lie. I *do* know what I expected to find, or hoped to find.

I hoped to find a plain ordinary hill with nothing but dirty snow and bare bushes on it. Then I could tell myself that I'd just imagined the whole thing. The hole in the hill, Mrs. F., Andrea, all of it— just like I'd imagined that dog lying on me.

And if I'd imagined the whole thing, well, then, I obviously did need more exercise, just like my mom was always saying. I needed to tire out my body and rest my tired brain. I *would* go out for hockey. I'd let myself get bodychecked into oblivion, and I'd let my mom and my dad get on with being unhappy. And I'd let Andrea get on with her eating and staring and pooping, which was obviously all she really wanted to do anyway.

There was nothing strange about the Monkey Paths at all. It hadn't snowed since the last time I'd been there, so there were a few more ski trails and a lot more piles of dog poop. But otherwise it was just the same.

It was just the same, except for a lot of goose yelping that was coming from somewhere beyond the clouds that filled the sky. Oh, and one other thing. There was this little kid there, all alone in the bushes.

24·The Same Place but Different

Some mother wasn't going to be happy about that. Little kids shouldn't be all alone in the bushes, as we have all been told again and again.

"Hi," I said, not expecting any answer except maybe "My-mommy-says-not-to-talk-to-strangers-so-go-away-and-leave-me-alone." That's what *I* used to say whenever older people tried to talk to me. I mean, they tell you not to talk to strangers, right? They tell it to you a lot. And for this kid, I was a stranger.

But the kid didn't seem to care.

"You can't have it," she said.

At least I think it was a she. It's hard to tell when they're wearing all those snowsuits and hats and scarves and all.

"Have what?" I said.

"The horn. I saw it first, so it's mine."

"What horn?"

"That one." She pointed to exactly the spot where I'd seen that hole in the side of the hill. "See?"

I did see. It was a bright-yellow horn. It looked like gold, except it obviously wasn't, of course. It had to be a plastic toy some kid had forgotten and left there. Maybe some kind of space toy.

I definitely did not need any space toy. "Go ahead, kid," I said. "It's all yours if you want it."

"Of course it is," she said calmly. "I saw it first."

And she waddled over to get it.

As she bent over to pick the horn up, those geese were getting louder and louder. The sky seemed to be full of barking, howling, screeching, screaming dogs.

I looked up. And I saw them.

They weren't geese. They weren't dogs either. Or, at least, not quite dogs.

They were dogs with human heads—great huge dogs with human heads and wildly shining human eyes and flying human hair and fangs. Sharp-pointed dog fangs in human mouths, glistening with saliva.

And those dogs were yelping to beat the band.

"No!" I shouted to the kid. "Don't blow it!" Why I don't know, but somehow I knew those dogs had something to do with the horn, that blowing it was definitely not going to be a good idea.

I ran over to the kid and grabbed the horn out of her hand. It was heavy, not plastic after all. The yelping overhead got a little less loud.

But the kid was furious. "It's mine," she said. "You're nasty. You're just a mean big kid and I'm going to tell my mommy on you. You'll be sorry. It's mine!"

And before I even knew what she was doing, the little devil gave me a big shove, and I fell over into the snow. Then she grabbed the horn right out of my hand and ran off with it.

When she got just out of my reach, she stopped, turned around, and gave me this big smirk. "So there!" she said. "And I can blow it if I want to, mister, because it's mine!"

Then she stuck the horn in her mouth and blew. A horrible groan came out of the horn.

And as the horn groaned, the yelping got louder, louder, louder, and I could see those dogs coming down at us out of the sky. As I finally pulled myself to my feet, I could see the sickening mad gleam in their eyes and the slobber coming out of their mouths. And as I tried to move forward, I could feel claws at the back of my head.

I lunged at the kid. I bodychecked her. And then I blacked out.

The next thing I knew, I was blinking at that hill again. And my head hurt like hell. I guess I'd maybe been knocked out. But now everything seemed okay. No dogs. No horn. And no kid.

No kid? I sat up, wincing at the pain in my head, and looked around. Yes, there she was, over by that tree.

She was lying on the ground, facedown in the center of a patch of snow that was all rucked up. It looked as if someone, or something, had been ripping at it.

Those claws. Those teeth.

My God, what had they done to her?

I tried not to think about the claws and the teeth as I pulled myself to my knees and crawled over to her body. I closed my eyes and then reached out to turn her over.

"You keep your hands off me, you . . . you meanie!"

And she sat up and slapped my arm away from her shoulder.

Thank God. She was okay.

She was fine, in fact. Apparently I was the one who was in trouble. As soon as she saw my face, she started to pummel me. It was amazing how much power she had in those cute little fists. And the whole time she was hitting me, she kept shrieking.

"You meanie! You hit me! You pushed me over! I'm telling!"

As I tried to keep those dangerous fists out of my face, I thought about what she was saying. It was true, I guess. Somehow I'd managed to push her over and out of the way of those dogs, or whatever they were.

I'd saved her. I was a hero.

And this was the thanks I was getting.

As if that wasn't bad enough, the air was suddenly filled with sirens. It was three cop cars screaming to a stop up on Churchill Drive. And an ambulance, too. And then some other cars—reporters, as it turned out. Apparently someone had heard all the yelping and seen those things coming for us and called 911. So now this little monster was going to rat on me to the fuzz, and I was going to be arrested for child molesting or something, right on TV. My mother was going to kill me.

As it turned out, I wasn't arrested, because some mother with a kid on a toboggan over by the hill had seen those dogs coming for us. She'd shouted at them, and that was probably why they'd decided to leave so suddenly, before actually starting on their tasty meal. So the cops didn't buy the kid's story, thank goodness. They were even nice enough to pull her off me and save me from certain physical damage.

"It's those damn strays," one of them told the reporters after the cops finished asking me some questions. I had decided not to be exactly truthful about my answers. The woman who called 911 had reported just a pack of wild dogs, and I wasn't about to tell any public official that the dogs had come zooming out of the air. Or that they had had human faces. That would be a first-class ticket to the booby hatch.

So strays it was. We all agreed. Everyone had been hearing them, the cops said, and it was getting serious. Something sure had to be done about them.

Something sure did.

The cops also told me how brave I was, and told the little girl with the fists that she should thank me.

Fat chance. She wasn't buying any. "He knocked me over!" she said. "And he stole my horn!" She gave me this incredibly dirty look.

So I told the cops about how I'd seen her playing with that horn before the dogs came. We searched the whole area for it. No horn. As the cops bundled the kid off to their car to drive her home, she gave me yet another dark look over her shoulder.

She was still convinced I'd stolen her stupid toy. So much for gratitude.

And so much for forgetting about the whole thing, like I'd planned.

Strays, the cop had said. Wild dogs on the loose. But I knew it wasn't dogs. Not ordinary dogs, anyway.

Nobody was going to believe me. Nobody was going to help me. But I had to do something.

I had to do something, and I was going to do it. Just as soon as I could figure out what it was.

Five

The next morning was bright and sunny—the kind of deceptively cheerful-looking winter day when it's cold enough outside to make you feel like a hero for being willing to live in Winnipeg at all. The kind of day when it's hard to imagine things like killer dogs, or geese, or whatever they were.

It was a relief not to be able to imagine them. It felt good. I ran down the stairs two at a time, all set to enjoy breakfast.

"I'm starving," I said to my mom, who was standing at the sink washing some dishes. "How about some bacon?"

"Bacon?" She turned and gave me this look. "After all that oatmeal? You must be joking."

"Oatmeal," I said, bewildered. "What oatmeal?"

That look Mom was giving me turned very strange. She pointed to the table. "*That* oatmeal, of course. The oatmeal you've been gulping down for the past ten minutes as if you hadn't even *seen* food for ten years."

Me, eating oatmeal? What was she talking about?

"And as if that wasn't bad enough," she went on, "all of a sudden you leap up as if you'd heard a ghost on the stairway and zoom! Off you go without even saying excuse me. And now you come darting back in here again, and you want bacon! Well, you can just forget about bacon. I can't afford to feed you breakfast more than once a day." And she turned back to the sink.

I still didn't know what she was talking about.

"But I'm hungry," I said. "I haven't eaten anything, honestly, Mom. You know I haven't, I—"

She slammed down the dish she'd been drying and headed toward the hallway.

"Nothing? So now eight or nine bowls of oatmeal is nothing? Heaven help me, I've given birth to a walking stomach! A food vacuum! Well, I give up. If you're still hungry, have more oatmeal. Have *all* the oatmeal! Eat me out of house and home! But," she added darkly as she made her way out the door, "no bacon."

I stood there with my mouth hanging open,

trying to figure it out. Mom seemed to have the idea that I'd been downstairs and had breakfast already—and that I'd eaten oatmeal.

I hate oatmeal.

It made no sense at all. Unless, of course, it was *them* again.

Them. Strangers. All at once my good feelings evaporated. Of course it was them. Not only had they stolen my sister and killed Mrs. F. and attacked some perfectly innocent kid in the park, but now they were making sure I didn't even get any breakfast.

It made me furious.

But I had to eat. I was starving. So I actually went over to the stove and spooned out a bowl of that disgusting goop and sat down to eat it. I poured enough milk over the oatmeal to hide it from view and grabbed the newspaper that was lying on the table. I hoped it would distract me from the cruel and unusual punishment going on inside my mouth.

It did. It was the big color picture on the front page that did it. It showed a bunch of cows.

That's right, cows. No bloodstained scene of an axe murder, no sexy woman in a bikini. Not the usual junk at all. Just cows.

Well, after the last few interesting days of my life, an axe murder would have seemed ho-hum. But cows were different. It caught my attention. I turned to page three like the paper said, to find out more.

From page three I learned that scientists were trying to figure out why cows on farms near

Winnipeg were producing milk that was deficient in nutrients. All the milk produced within about two hundred kilometers of the city was affected. It looked like milk and tasted like milk, but tests showed that it had no food value. As usual, different scientists had a number of theories to explain why, all of them contradicting each other.

As if that wasn't bad enough, I turned the page only to discover a story about those creatures in the park—with my name in it. There was no picture, thank God, but the words made up for it. They didn't spare any of the juicy details, and the reporter made a big fuss about what a brave young man I was, a sterling example to today's degenerate youth.

As if that oatmeal wasn't enough to make me feel nauseous.

The scene outside school was hectic. There must have been about thirty cars on that one short block of Hay, trying to pull up and park outside the front doors. There were horns beeping and tires squealing, and all these kids were getting out of the cars in the middle of the street and laughing and yelling at each other as they tried to make it over to the sidewalk without getting creamed. It was madness. What was going on here?

As I made my way through the crowd and up to the front door, I heard this voice calling me. "Hey, Nesbit," it said. "Think you're some big hero, eh?"

Damn. It was Jason Garrett, lurking there just

waiting to pounce on me. Garrett is this dumb-jock hockey player. I mean, really dumb, much worse than my buds Mark and Rob. For him, bodychecking is a daily hallway activity. He'd obviously seen that stupid article in the paper, and the body he had chosen for today's target practice was going to be mine.

Well, I'd sort of expected that. The surprising thing was finding out that the dumb jock actually knew how to read.

"Bug off, Jase," I shouted at him over the noise of car horns and squealing tires. I tried to keep a lot of people between us as I headed toward the door.

But once Jase makes up his so-called mind, he's unstoppable—like a cement truck with no brakes. Before I knew it, three girls and a couple of guys were sprawled on the sidewalk, their books flying in all directions. Jase had made his usual elegant move through the crowd, and he was punching me on the arm.

"Some scene, eh, big hero? Makes you proud, eh?" He punched my arm again.

"Me, proud? What are you talking about?" I tried to push his hand away, but he kept right on punching.

"Yeah, you. It's all your fault, right?"

"What are you talking about? And stop hitting me, you creep."

Jase looked down at his hand and got this surprised look on his face, as if his brain hadn't even known what his hand was doing—assuming, of course, that there actually *was* a brain in there under the concrete. "Oh, sorry," he said in a thoughtless sort of way. "I should have known your poor little arm couldn't take it." Then his eyes lit up. "Anyway," he crowed, "you know what I mean. That story in the paper about what a big hero you are. Eh, hero?" He made a fist and moved it toward my arm again, then saw the look in my eyes, changed his mind—and swatted me across the butt.

"Cut it out," I said, trying to move a few steps out of range. "So what about it?"

"So all the parents are worried about those wild dogs, and they're scared to let their kids walk to school by themselves. So they're driving them here. That's why all these cars. My dad even made *me* come with him in the car."

Jeez, his dad must be even dumber than him, if he actually thought those dog creatures stood a chance against a ruthless hulk like Jase.

Anyway, I was rubbing my sore butt with one hand and my sore arm with the other. This is not an easy thing to do: try it sometime. Meanwhile, Jase stood there looking out over the street, and this huge smile grew on his dumb face. "Isn't it a mess? Isn't it great? I love it!"

Then he turned back to me and punched my arm again. "But jeez, Nesbit, it must have been something with those dogs, eh? What did they look like, really? Were their eyes wild? Were their teeth sharp?"

I didn't say anything. I wasn't about to tell anybody about those weird human faces.

But by this time a whole bunch of other guys had gathered around. Even Rob and Mark were there. Well, it's not often I get everybody's attention like that, and I guess I should have been enjoying it. But every time somebody asked another question, I would see those dogs and their grotesque human faces, and once more I'd find myself imagining what that kid would have looked like if I hadn't managed to shove her out of the way.

"Look, you guys," I said in my iciest voice as I gave them my iciest glare, "I really don't want to talk about it."

"Oh, yeah, big hero," said Jase. "You just wanna keep all the gory details to yourself." Then he made his move, but that time, for once, I managed to get out of range just before the punch landed on my arm.

"Look," I said angrily, "it wasn't anything. Nothing. I was just walking in the park, and I . . . I heard this noise, right, and I saw these dogs and this kid. And . . . and that's all," I finished lamely.

"But what did they look like?" somebody asked. "What did the *dogs* look like?" And then everybody asked questions all at once.

"Really," I said, "it was just this kid is all. She blew into that horn and—"

Oops. I didn't want to say anything about the horn. I don't know why, exactly, but for some reason

I just didn't want anybody to know about the horn.

"Horn?" An urgent voice cut through all the laughter. It was Liam Green, which was really odd. Liam was this really quiet kid who hardly ever said anything to anybody. I mean, he'd been in my class for two years and I hardly even knew him. I don't think I'd ever heard him say more than three words, and here he was pushing through a whole crowd of guys and asking a question, looking a little scared but as if he was determined to know the answer. Weird.

"What horn?" he asked.

"Oh, nothing, it was just a plastic horn, a toy. I guess the kid was playing with it or something."

"Forget the dumb horn. Tell us about the teeth," said Jase. "Tell us about the saliva-dripping fangs!" And damned if he didn't punch my arm *again*.

Fortunately the bell rang just then, and I took the opportunity to get out of there as fast as I could. My arm needed a rest.

If it had happened to somebody else, I guess I would have been right in there asking questions, too. Funny how interesting blood and guts and horror are until you actually get close to seeing some.

As I headed off through the crowd and into school, I had to pass right by Liam Green. And as I went by, he gave me this piercing stare.

It was as if he wanted to see right through my face into my brain.

Six

I spent all day avoiding question after question about those dogs in the park, and feeling nauseous every time somebody brought it up and made the whole ugly mess pop into my head again.

What was even worse, after every class and all through lunch, wherever I happened to be and whoever happened to be talking to me, Liam Green would be there, not saying anything, just staring that weird stare at me.

It was real creepy. In comparison, it was even kind of comforting to listen to my social studies teacher, Mr. Foley, drone on about how people in Japan are really just like us, except, of course, when they're eating raw fish and committing suicide in fancy ways.

After school I went out the Arnold Street door, partly to get away from everybody else and partly to avoid the traffic jam that had developed again out front. And then, instead of just going down Casey the way we guys all usually go, I headed over to Fisher, one block over. I wanted to be by myself.

I'd made it all the way to Fisher Park, not far from home and safety, when suddenly someone popped out from behind a tree and blocked the sidewalk in front of me.

It was Liam Green.

Now this was really wild. Here's this shy guy who says nothing to me for two whole years, even though we often sit almost beside each other in class and even though I do try to say a few words to him myself now and then, just for the sake of politeness. Now all of a sudden he's not only talking—he's threatening me. It's like the mild-mannered reporter Clark Kent suddenly turning into Superman.

Although the way he was trembling, he still looked more like Clark Kent.

"What do *you* want, Green?" I said. "Let me by."

"No," he said in a high-pitched whine. "I won't let you by. Not until you tell me about the horn."

The horn? The horn in the park? What business was it of his? Like I said, I hardly knew the guy. And anyway, I wasn't about to be pushed around by any Clark Kent.

"It's too bloody cold out here to stand around

chatting about stupid horns," I said. "Let me by." I began to push my way past him.

Liam grabbed my jacket. "I *have* to know," he whined. "You *have* to tell me."

I didn't have to tell anybody anything. I shoved his hand off my jacket and stomped off down the street.

"Please," I heard him calling after me, "all you have to do is say yes or no. That's all. Was it a long gold horn with a curved black handle? Just yes or no."

I stopped in midstep, surprised. The horn *was* long. The handle *was* black and curved. I turned around and looked back at him.

"It was, wasn't it?" he repeated, glaring into my face with fiery eyes.

I glared right back, not saying anything. For some reason I didn't want to tell him. I don't know why, exactly. I mean, what difference could it make whether or not I answered his question?

But then, all these *things* had been happening to me. Scary things. Things I couldn't understand. And now little old Liam Green was acting so odd. How did I know I could trust him?

"It was," he said, nodding, suddenly certain. "It had to be. And the kid blew on it, didn't she?"

So he knew that, too, did he? Suddenly I gave in. Hell, what did I have to lose? He seemed to know already anyway. And it was just Liam Green, after all, just a kid in my school.

So I told him.

"Yes," I said. "If you must know. She did. She did blow on it. And then—" Inside my mind, I was seeing a picture of those creatures again.

"And then," said Liam, "*they* came. She called them, and they came. The Strangers."

Strangers.

As he said that word, I suddenly remembered Mrs. F. sitting there inside the hill with Andrea on her lap and saying, "It's them. It's the Strangers." I shivered, and not just from the cold.

Meanwhile, Liam was looking at me in this weird way—waiting, I guessed, to see if I knew what he was talking about.

I knew, all right.

"Strangers," I said. "You mean . . ." Well, why not just say it and get it over with. "You mean . . . fairies? You know about the fairies?"

Liam suddenly looked furious. "Yes," he said angrily, "fairies. I know about them, all right. But the important thing is you know about them, too. And if you know about them, you need my help."

Well, I really did need some help. I sure wasn't getting very far in this saving-Andrea business by myself.

But what help could Liam Green give me? It didn't make any sense.

A thought suddenly occurred to me. "Anyway," I said, "how do *you* know about them? I mean, until a few days ago, I'd never even heard of the Strangers."

Liam squirmed uncomfortably, and looked at me, and said nothing.

"I can't," he said in a tiny voice, looking down at the ground. "I just can't tell you. Please don't ask me."

That made me really mad. "Jeez, Green," I said. "You're really something. You pop out at me from behind a tree like some demented sex maniac, you grab onto my clothes, you insist I tell you things—and you won't tell *me* anything. Just forget it," I said, and began to stomp off again.

"No," he wailed, pulling on my jacket yet again. "I'll tell you."

So I stopped and waited.

I waited for a long time as Liam stood there looking upset and confused. "It's like this," he finally said in a low voice. "I know about them . . . because . . ."

He still hesitated, as if he was desperately afraid to say what he had to say next. But finally, he spoke.

"I know about them because I *am* one. A Stranger. Now you know. I'm a fairy."

I just stared at him. I didn't know what to say.

He looked like any normal kid—a little skinny and short, maybe, but normal.

Although when I thought about it, he hadn't always looked so normal.

I was beginning to remember what had happened when Liam first arrived in our class last year. I was remembering how everyone laughed when Mme. Mackenzie said his name was Green, because he did look sort of green. I mean, his skin really was kind of greenish.

People made fun of him about it for a while,

until it became clear that Liam wasn't going to get mad or cry or fight or anything. He just sat there quietly and took it. Teasing someone like that just wasn't any fun, and eventually everyone lost interest and left him alone. Even that turkey Jason stopped bugging him.

Now, I could see, his skin was just ordinary skin like mine, and I realized he hadn't looked at all greenish for a long time.

So now Liam was just a normal kid with normal skin, wearing a normal if kind of geeky parka and normal blue jeans. As far as I could tell, he didn't have wings. And I'd never noticed him making magic wishes and sprinkling sparkly fairy dust in the corridors of Churchill High.

But normal kids do not stand in the middle of the district of Riverview in the middle of the city of Winnipeg on a sunny and very cold day in the last decade of the twentieth century and calmly announce to another kid that they are fairies.

So maybe he wasn't so normal after all. Maybe I shouldn't be talking to him. Maybe it wasn't safe.

"You're crazy," I said. "Let me by."

"I wish I was crazy," he said. "But unfortunately, it's true. I'm a fairy. And I can prove it to you."

"Prove it to me? What, are you going to take out your magic wand and change me into a frog or something?"

That made Liam look even angrier than he had already—which was pretty damn angry. I could see his fists clenching inside his mittens.

"Sorry," I said. "It was just a joke."

"Yeah, sure," Liam said grumpily. "Some joke. You wouldn't think it was so funny if *you* were a fairy."

"I *said* I was sorry."

"Okay, okay. So you're sorry. Look, what *do* you know about us anyway? About fairies, I mean?"

"Almost nothing. And let me tell you," I added, getting a little hot about it, "that's more than I want to know. I was better off when I thought fairies were cute little imaginary creatures that spent their time sitting around on toadstools and thinking happy thoughts about friendship and rainbows." I was remembering a horrible experience with some so-called poetry that they'd made us read back around grade two.

"Yes, I know," he said, with this sad look on his face. Apparently he'd read those dumb poems, too. "How people get away with spreading those disgusting lies is beyond me. Talk about racism! Anyway," he went on, "if you know anything about us at all, then you know there's just one way to tell us from humans. That's the proof."

"Nostrils," I said, suddenly remembering my conversation with Mrs. F. "Fairies are supposed to have just one nostril."

"That's it," said Liam. "That's how you can

tell." And now he looked really embarrassed and sort of hid his head in his scarf. He knew he had to show me, and it was obvious he didn't want to. I could see that for him it was like having to take a shower after swimming class before your hair grows.

But he did it anyway. He blushed bright red, and then he sort of gulped and bent his head back in the bright sunlight. And there I was, staring straight into the bottom of his nose.

At first it looked perfectly normal—two holes, just like everybody else. But then I looked closer, and I could see that one of the holes was fake. It ended a little bit inside, the passage totally blocked by solid skin.

It was true, it was really true.

Liam had just one nostril.

He *was* a fairy.

Just one nostril—the kind of thing you'd never notice unless someone wanted you to.

"I give up," I said, feeling defeated. "You win. You're a fairy, all right. This nose business—it must save a lot of Kleenex when you have a cold."

Well, I couldn't help being snarky, the way I was feeling by then. It was as if everybody in the whole world had decided to gang up and play this mammoth practical joke on me all at the same time. Fairies on Fisher Street. As if the dogs with human faces weren't enough.

But then I immediately felt bad about it. I

mean, it wasn't his fault he was a fairy, right?

"Oops," I said. "I'm sorry. It just—"

"I know," he said, his hand held up over his nose as if to hide it from my view. "That's why I keep it to myself. And," he added fiercely, "why *you'd* better keep it to yourself. Or else."

Or else what?

And then I remembered he wasn't your usual sort of wimp. He was one of *them*. Anything could happen. Maybe he'd turn into a flying dog and bite my throat out.

"Don't worry," I said. "I'm not saying anything to anybody. I'm not *that* dumb."

Not that I was really afraid of him. But I could just imagine how Mark or Rob or, God forbid, that creep Jase would respond to my announcement that a kid in our class was a fairy.

"But that horn," I said, suddenly remembering how this conversation with a fairy had started. "Those dogs flying out of the sky. Why—?"

"It was the Sky Yelpers," Liam said in a mournful voice.

"Sky Yelpers? I thought you said they were Strangers."

"They are, sort of. The Yelpers are a special kind of Strangers. But we're not all like them. You can't judge us all by their actions."

I was glad to hear that. Really glad. Maybe Liam wouldn't bite my head off after all. I nodded at him, and he continued.

"I thought it might be Yelpers because of all the barking. They often take the form of dogs, see? And when I heard about the horn, well, then, I knew for sure. It's the horn that calls them. 'Foolish is he who blows the horn of the Hunter.'"

"Foolish isn't the word for it," I said, "if what they tried to do to that kid in the park means anything." There was silence for a few moments as we thought about it.

"That's why I had to warn you," Liam finally said. "If you were there, it wasn't by accident. It never is. You were meant to be there. You're part of it, somehow. Hell," he added angrily, looking up into the cloudless sky. "It's probably not even safe for me to be talking to you like this, now that they've got your scent."

What did the little creep mean by that? Surely they wouldn't . . . ? I looked up too, swinging my head wildly in all directions. Nothing there, thank God.

Meanwhile, Liam was still talking. "It's not the only thing either, is it? You've had something else happen. You must have, because you called us Strangers. You knew our real name. And you knew about our nostrils."

He was right. It wasn't the only thing, not by a long shot. And it would be a relief to talk to somebody about it, somebody who wouldn't just laugh or think I was nuts.

So I did. I told him everything. I told him about Mrs. F. and about Andrea. I even told him about my nightmare about the dog lying on me.

"That was a hag," he said. "A hag was riding you."

"A hag? Like a witch, you mean? But it wasn't a hag. It was a dog, and anyway, it wasn't real, it was a dream. I woke up again, and—"

"No," he insisted. "It was real. It was a hag. They come at night and sit on your chest and try to squeeze the breath out of you. It must have been part of the pack of Yelpers. If you're being hag-ridden, then they're after you for sure." He took a quick look up into the sky again.

"But why?" I asked, looking up, too. Still nothing there. "Why me? I haven't done anything."

"Maybe not," he said. "But after the window in the hill opened, you'd had contact with the Strangers. So they had your scent. That little girl in the park was probably just an innocent bystander. The Hunter left his horn for *you* to find. He probably hoped you'd see it and pick it up, that you couldn't resist blowing it."

"But what does blowing it do? I don't get it."

"It's a signal, see? Blowing on that horn calls down the Sky Yelpers. The horn called them to the feast, and so they came, and—" He paused, unwilling to say what came next.

I said it for him. "And feasted."

"Yes. Or at least, they tried to. They tried to eat you. And," he added, this weird wild smile on his face, "they'll probably try it again."

Seven

So I was supposed to be a meal for some flying doggies. Johnny Nesbit Brand Yelper Chow, for contented cannibal canines.

I guess I ought to have been scared out of my wits. But somehow I wasn't. I was . . . well, I was relieved. I mean, there I'd been, thinking I was all alone in this mess. And now I wasn't alone anymore. I had Liam. And sure, maybe he looked like just a wimpy little kid who hadn't been getting his daily requirement of protein, but he was a Stranger. A genuine fairy.

Liam told me about it as we walked toward my house, speaking in this intense angry voice as if his life story were my fault somehow. But the words still poured out of him. I guess having someone to talk to about this weird stuff was just as much of a relief for him as it was for me. Hell, he was concentrating so hard on telling me about it all that he didn't look up into the sky more than ten or fifteen times the whole way.

Liam told me he came here from Stranger country a couple of years ago. He could hardly remember it, but he thought he was a shepherd there, or something like that. One day he followed his animals down into a flat valley with a river flowing through it. He went inside a cave by the edge of the river—because he thought maybe one of the animals had strayed into the cave. And he got lost in the darkness.

When he finally found his way out, it wasn't where he'd gone in. It was colder and brighter than any place he'd ever been. It was here. He'd come out on the river by Churchill Drive Park. The cave in their country was a storm sewer outlet in ours—the sewer outlet in the riverbank just under the pumphouse, down at the end of the park.

"This park must be a doorway," Liam said. "It's a place where the two countries meet. That's probably why these things keep happening here in Riverview."

Anyway, Liam had wandered around on the frozen river, half frozen himself, until someone spotted him and called 911. But even after he was rushed into the hospital, he couldn't eat anything the people there tried to feed him, and he'd nearly starved to death. Luckily, this guy named Rhymer showed up, and he told the doctors what Liam could eat.

"Who was he?" I asked. "And how did he know?"

Mr. Rhymer was his foster father—the man he

lived with now, in one of those big old houses over on Ashland, a few blocks up from my place. Rhymer was a specialist in folklore, a professor at the University of Winnipeg downtown, and he'd only heard about Liam by accident through some gossip. The cops had kept it out of the papers, because they thought people might get excited about Martians landing or something, and start to panic.

But somehow, of course, people got to know anyway, and so this Rhymer guy heard about it and investigated. And when he finally talked the cops into showing him Liam's picture, he knew right away where Liam had come from.

It was the green skin that tipped him off. The color was really intense at first—like leaves or grass in summer. The cops thought it had to be frostbite, but Mr. Rhymer knew better. So he arranged to come to the hospital—not without a lot of trouble from the cops, who couldn't figure out how a folklore specialist, of all things, was going to do any good. But then he suggested what to feed Liam, and by then the hospital people had run out of ideas of their own and they decided that his suggestion couldn't do any harm, so they tried it. And it worked, so the cops began to trust Mr. Rhymer a little more.

And also decided to keep the whole business quiet forever, because it was just too weird.

"Why?" I asked. "What was it he told them to feed you?"

Liam looked embarrassed. "It was . . . well, it was . . . green beans." He turned a bright red. "I know it's dumb, but Mr. Rhymer says it's all that a lot of the people eat in our country. That's what made me green, see? Since I've started to eat other foods, my skin has changed. And I hate green beans, now," he added urgently. "I never eat them."

As if I cared what he ate—just as long as it wasn't human flesh.

Anyway, Mr. Rhymer had got him to eat the beans and saved his life. And later, when it became clear to everybody that Liam had only these really vague memories of the past, and that he had no relatives and nowhere to go in our country, Rhymer had arranged with Children's Aid to have Liam live with him.

So it was true. He *was* a fairy.

I felt great. A fairy would know what to do. I could just put the whole thing into his hands. He'd save Andrea for me. He'd probably even save the world.

It felt so great that I decided not to remember what a puny little wimp Liam was. I decided not to remember how he kept looking up nervously into the sky the whole time he talked to me, and how he brushed vigorously on his parka every time I accidentally happened to touch it. I even decided not to remember that weird smile he gave me when he told me I was going to be Yelper Chow, as if he wasn't all that unhappy about it, as if the whole thing was my fault somehow and he was hoping I'd pay for it.

By the time we got to my place, the sun was beginning to sink. So we arranged to meet the next day after school, to make plans about what to do next. Liam said we had to find some public place where we could talk privately, so we wouldn't draw the attention of those Yelpers. The first place I thought of was the Safeway up on Osborne. Maybe it was all that talk about green beans.

Liam thought it was a terrific idea. "They'll never think of looking for us in a grocery store," he said, "and the food smells will confuse the scent."

Ah, yes, the scent. A good point. I wasn't finding it easy to remember that I was supposed to be thinking like a food product now. But even that didn't dampen my high spirits. As I headed toward the house, my head was full of wonderful pictures of all the wonderful ways Liam was going to save Andrea.

Maybe he and I would go off to the Monkey Paths, and I'd stand there and watch while he said a few magic words, and the hill would turn into a window again. Liam would shatter that invisible glass with one touch of his magic finger, and then we'd climb in and rescue Mrs. F. and Andrea.

Or maybe he'd just chant a spell—"Shazzam!"— and Mrs. F. and Andrea would simply materialize right before us, right there in Safeway.

Or maybe he'd wave his arms through the air and there'd be colored lights and a huge explosion, and dead dogs would fall out of the sky. And a huge orchestra would play happy music while a choir sang and fireworks exploded.

I mean, he was a fairy, wasn't he?

The next morning I had a visit from the hag again—that big dog, I mean—lying on me and suffocating me.

Only this time it didn't just pant. Just before I woke up, I could feel its teeth coming right through the sheet, beginning to tighten around my throat. And I couldn't call out. I couldn't do anything. I just had to lie there. I really thought I was a goner.

After I woke up the second time and the hag suddenly wasn't there anymore, I took a look at the sheet.

There were little holes in it. There was slobber on it.

It had been bitten. Bitten by real teeth.

The hag was real. Now I had no choice but to believe it.

And some people make do with an alarm clock.

It took about five minutes of lying in bed before my heart stopped pounding enough for me to get up. By that time Mom was on the warpath about how lazy I was. It looked like the beginning of another great day.

To top it all off, the newspaper was full of *them* again. The Strangers.

Or at least I guessed it was them. I mean, there were all these stories about weird things happening in Riverview. "The Neighborhood of Creepy Horrors—Would *You* Have the Guts to Live There?" one headline said.

The story was about a guy who was convinced that a whole bunch of trees on the riverbank in the park suddenly took off after him while he was out skiing at night. Willow trees. They howled at him and tried to catch him in their branches. They only gave up when he managed to get himself out of the dark and near the lights by the bridge.

He could have been drunk. Hey, when you look at the way those ski trails in the park swerve all over the place, you have to think that at least some of those skiers have to be drunk.

There was another story, too, about a house on Churchill Drive. It seems this one guy bought the house from another guy, and the other guy moved out. But when the new owner came to move in, he discovered the house had moved. The whole house. He claimed it was the other way around from the way it was when he'd bought it—the front was on the back and the back was on the front. Now instead of looking out at the park and the river, the big picture window in the living room showed a beautiful view of the garbage cans in the back lane. So the new owner was suing the former owner. But the former owner said the house was the right way around when he moved out and it wasn't his problem.

The reporter had also interviewed some of the neighbors. As far as they knew, the house was the right way around the night before, and it had already been moved when they woke up in the morning. Also, they were planning to complain to the mayor and to the city council and to their Member of Parliament about this flagrant violation of the zoning laws.

Well, so maybe all those people were drunk, too. Maybe an epidemic of alcoholism was sweeping the neighborhood.

Or maybe it was them. The Strangers.

Somehow, that was beginning to seem more logical.

Before heading off for school, I hit Mom up for my allowance. It was Friday, and she owed me.

What a mistake *that* was.

"Look here, young man," she said. "I already told you that I don't see the humor in this so-called joke of yours. I was angry enough yesterday, but this is worse. You know full well I gave you your allowance not five minutes ago."

"But . . . but . . ." Well, there was nothing to say, was there? It was obviously one of *them* again, playing some stupid trick. I headed off to school stony broke and in a deep fit of depression.

I spent most of the morning in a daze. Liam avoided me like the plague, glaring at me and quickly looking down at his work whenever I happened to look up at him. Why was *he* mad at *me? My* relatives weren't trying to steal *his* allowance. *My* relatives weren't trying to have *him* for lunch.

I guess he just hated the fact that I knew his secret. He didn't seem to like being a Stranger all that much.

The big thrill of the day was language arts,

the last class of the morning. Milton introduced a guest speaker—a kid named Rebecca something or other, from Montrose School. She was on some kind of campaign about stopping nuclear war and she was going around visiting all the schools in the city. I mean, as if Sky Yelpers and allowance thieves weren't enough, I had to worry about nuclear annihilation also. And besides which, the room was really stuffy and I felt depressed and overheated. I rushed outside for a breath of fresh air as soon as Milton let us go.

I rushed out only to see somebody pushing around a little girl on the sidewalk in front of the school. A really little girl—I guess she was on her way home for lunch from Riverview School, which is a couple of blocks away from Churchill. Anyway, the little girl was crying and cringing because this guy was pushing her around.

This guy who looked a lot like me.

And when I say a lot, I'm not kidding. I would have sworn it *was* me, if I hadn't been the one who was looking at this guy who looked like me. Same handsome face I see in the mirror every morning, same hunky body, even the same ski jacket and high-tops and all.

An exact duplicate.

It was not a pleasant sight. Seeing myself pushing around a little kid really upset me. I hate bullies.

So I rushed over to grab the person who looked just like me, only to see him sort of blink out.

Like a light turning off. Shazzam, and he was gone.

It startled me so much that I just stood there and stared. Which meant the only person standing by the frightened little girl was me. The real me.

The little girl just stood there screaming as that Rebecca kid with the nuclear war came out of the building. She took one glance at what was going on, and she came bounding down the sidewalk like a cat after a mouse and stared at me as if her eyes had daggers in them. Then she gave me this lecture about how bullies cause war—a lecture from a stupid kid my own age who thought she knew everything, but who from the evidence of this heated discussion did not seem to understand the basic principles of non-violence.

And, of course, she ratted on me, and I ended up having a cute little talk with the principal for most of the afternoon, about nastiness and bullying and all.

And dogs were yowling off in the distance through the whole thing. By the time I got through the rest of the afternoon, I was more than ready for my rendezvous at the Safeway. I wanted Liam to get those Strangers for me. I wanted it bad.

Eight

"Of course it was Strangers," said Liam impatiently, looking furtively over his shoulder as he tossed a bag of prunes into the cart. "What did you think it was? Martians?"

The two of us were strolling through Safeway as we talked, loading up a cart and trying to look like ordinary Friday-afternoon shoppers. Not very successfully, though. Liam spent so much time glancing nervously around in all directions that even the most genial grocery-store manager in all of North America would have to suspect the little wimp was planning some major five-finger bargain hunting.

And if that weren't enough, the groceries Liam and I were randomly picking up as we made our way down the aisles and concentrated on our conversation didn't look all that much like any ordinary diet. So far we had a king-size jar of sauerkraut, three bags of frozen asparagus tips, a huge hunk of raw liver wrapped up in plastic, ten tubes of Preparation H, six cans of anchovy fillets, and the prunes. It was like gourmet night at the Masochists' Club.

Anyway, according to Liam, I'd been right about all that stuff in the newspaper—the milk having no nutritional value and the house being moved and the trees chasing people and all. That was the kind of stuff Strangers were famous for.

Liam also explained about the bully in the playground who looked like me. "That was a Cowalker," he said, stopping the cart just long enough to reach up to a high shelf and lift down a couple of boxes of instant oatmeal.

Well, Preparation H and raw liver I could live with, but there *are* limits. I took the oatmeal from him and put it back up on the shelf as I listened to him.

Cowalkers. It seems that they're a special kind of Stranger, a kind that steals people's images. This Cowalker had probably stolen my image from the mirror one morning while I was putting gel in my hair or something. After that it could look like me whenever it wanted to.

It must have been the same Cowalker that ate all the oatmeal and bummed my allowance off my mom.

The creep owed me five bucks.

But according to Liam, that Cowalker wasn't my main problem. Not by a long shot.

"No," he said. "It's those Sky Yelpers you really need to worry about. They don't just steal images, see? With them it's whole bodies. They aren't all that fussy about *what* bodies, either. Animals, humans, they don't really care. Any old corpse will do, and if they can't find one, well, they just *make* one."

Apparently that group in the park had concentrated on stealing the corpses of dogs.

"At least so far," Liam added.

So far? What did that mean? It took me a while to figure it out.

Me. He was thinking of me. If I didn't watch my step, it might be *my* body flying over the park in search of tasty kiddie meals.

My body, but the me inside would be long gone. The distant memory of a good meal.

"Jeez," I said, "you Strangers do have some bad habits, don't you?"

Liam suddenly stopped smiling, and his eyes blazed. "Now look here, Nesbit," he said angrily, his fists clenching, "you just watch your step. Ordinary Strangers are *not* vicious like Sky Yelpers."

Not vicious, eh? The way he was looking at that moment he sure could have fooled me.

And besides which, it seems that so-called "ordinary" Strangers turned houses around and stole people's allowances. Apparently Liam's idea of being vicious was not quite the same as mine.

But I had to trust him. He was all I had.

So I gave him what I hoped was a reassuring nod, and after a bit he unclenched his fists and calmed down a little and went on to tell me that Sky Yelpers weren't really Strangers at all. They were the souls of dead humans. Humans like me, but *bad* ones who did evil things in their lives and never repented, so they had to live on after their moldering corpses for eternity. Apparently the *real* Strangers looked down on them because they'd been humans once. And that wasn't their only problem, either. They hated to be disembodied. That's why they wandered the worlds under the leadership of the Hunter, the guy with the horn, killing creatures and stealing their bodies.

"So Yelpers are nothing like Strangers, see? *Nothing!*"

I still wasn't sure I could see what the big difference was. But Liam obviously thought it was important, because by this time his voice had risen to a loud whine—so loud that a woman who was standing near us looking at the household cleaners was startled by it, and nearly dropped the bottle of Lysol she was holding. She stared angrily at Liam, and he blushed bright red.

We were definitely not doing a good job of being unobtrusive.

I hastily pushed the cart around the corner and into the next aisle, out of sight of that angry woman.

"And anyway," Liam went on indignantly as he chased me around the corner, still seething, "I'm not a Stranger anymore. Not really. Now that I live here, I've stopped being a fairy. That's what my foster father, Mr. Rhymer, says. It's the food, he says. He's an expert, so he should know. I'm *human* now, just like you."

Human, maybe—but just like me? As I looked

at his flushed face, I couldn't help thinking that according to him, those Yelpers were humans, too. I just nodded back at him from over my shoulder as I tossed some canned turnips into the cart.

Meanwhile, Liam was still ranting away. "Just like you. Because if I *was* still a Stranger, do you think I'd even be here talking to you like this? Trying to help you? Fat chance. A Stranger wouldn't help, no way. Strangers don't give a damn about others. Not other Strangers, and certainly not human beings like you. But I do give a damn. I care about people just as much as you do, Nesbit. And you'd better believe it, or I'll . . . I'll . . ."

He stopped in midsentence, apparently unable to think of any act of terrorism suitably violent enough to express his deep human caring. His fists were clenched, and his eyes were glinting again. For a little wimp he looked pretty horrible. Pretty vicious. I decided to at least pretend to believe it. I gave him another nod as I unthinkingly placed some more cans of vegetables into the cart.

"AIEEE!"

I nearly jumped out of my skin. What now? It was Liam, of course, acting unobtrusive by shrieking at the top of his voice.

As he screamed, that woman from the household cleaners in the last aisle was rounding the corner, and this time she was so startled that she rammed her cart into a display of canned pineapple. Cans of pineapple were rolling everywhere.

But Liam didn't even notice. He'd lunged for our cart as he screamed, and now I could see that he was desperately clawing around at the stuff in it. He finally emerged with the two cans of vegetables I'd just put there, one in each hand.

"We don't need these," he said with great distaste, waving them in my face and then stashing them on the nearest shelf. "We definitely do not need these."

I looked at those two cans.

Green beans.

I should have known.

And it wasn't as if green beans were really disgusting. Not like oatmeal, for instance.

By this time the household-cleaner woman was waving her finger in Liam's face.

"Now you look here, kid," she said. "If I hear you shrieking just one more time, I'm calling the manager. This is a grocery store, not a day care." And she stomped back to her cart, angrily kicking cans of pineapple out of her path.

That was enough. Quite enough.

"Look, Green," I said. "The idea was to keep a low profile. That's why we're here, remember? And every two seconds you do something else to draw attention to us. I'm beginning to wonder whose side you're on."

I was, too. But like I said, he was all I had. I needed him.

Andrea needed him.

So I gulped, and quickly went on. "Not really, of

course," I said. "I know you're on my side. Because you're human, right? Like me. Hell, anyone can see you're human."

As I said that, he nodded, and he did actually start to look more human.

"Just don't pick up any more green beans," he said grumpily. And he followed obediently along beside me as I quickly wheeled our cart away from all that dumped pineapple.

In the next aisle, Liam was calm enough to explain about Andrea.

It was a Stranger, of course. *Another* kind of Stranger, a sort of Cowalker except lazier. This one was called a Changeling.

"I asked Mr. Rhymer about it," Liam said. "He says it's probably not even an important Stranger—just a run-of-the-mill fairy with nothing much to do, some lazy good-for-nothing looking for a quiet life. So he was happy to get sent here. As long as that Stranger pretends to be your sister, it gets all the food and drink it wants, and it doesn't have to do anything but lie there all day and laugh at the way it's fooling you all."

I thought about it. Why us? Why was it sent in the first place, and who sent it?

Not that it mattered really. I asked Liam about what did matter. "So how can we stop it from fooling us? How can we get my parents to see it for what it is?"

"Well . . ." He paused for a moment. "There are different ways. Back in the old days when people suspected a baby was a Changeling, they sometimes just threw it into the fireplace. Or they'd heat up a red-hot shovel and then put the baby on it. The Changeling can't take the pain, and so it reveals itself. That's one way."

"Excuse me for living," I said, "but I'm not about to throw my sister into any fireplace. Not even if it's really some evil little monster that just looks like my sister. I won't."

"No," he said thoughtfully. "I guess I wouldn't either, if it was my sister. I mean, what if it wasn't a Changeling after all, just a perfectly normal baby that happened to have some disease or something? Then you'd feel bad, wouldn't you?" It was a real question. He looked as if he weren't really sure if he would or not.

"No, that wouldn't be a human thing to do. I wouldn't do it either, for sure." He sounded as if he were trying to talk himself into it. "Anyway," he went on in a breezier tone, "sometimes people used to show up a Changeling a different way. A lot of Strangers are vain, see, and they love to think about how stupid human beings are compared to them. So the people would do something really stupid. Like they'd take some eggshells and boil water in them in front of the Changeling."

"That's pretty stupid, all right," I said.

"Yeah. The Changeling would watch the water boiling in the eggshells until it couldn't bear it anymore. And then it'd stand up in its cradle and tell the people how dumb they were and give itself away."

I could do that. It was stupid, but I could do it.

"Where are the eggs?" I asked. "At the back of the store, aren't they, with the milk? Let's go get eggs."

I started to head for the back of the store where the dairy products were, but Liam held me back.

"Sorry," he said. "Mr. Rhymer says that probably wouldn't work nowadays. It's been done once too often. They know the trick already."

"Then . . ." I gulped. "Then Andrea is gone forever?"

"No. There's . . . well, there's one other way." He hesitated.

"Tell me," I said. "It can't be that bad."

It *was* that bad.

To begin with, I had to get something called fairy ointment. I had to get it and rub it on my mom's and dad's eyes. Then they'd see the Changeling for what it really was. It would have to go back to its own land, and the real Andrea could come home again.

Simple, that part was.

Except, guess what? They don't carry this fairy ointment stuff in the drug section at Safeway. Believe me, I checked.

No, there's just one place to get fairy ointment.

Stranger country.

And besides which, Liam said, I had to go to Stranger country anyway. I had to go there to find Andrea and Mrs. F., and I had to bring them back with me before I could even try that business with the ointment.

I had to go to Stranger country.

Well, so much for my vision of Liam waving a wand and saying shazzam and all.

Apparently, the person who was going to have to do something about it all was, guess who.

Me. Just little old human being me.

Nine

So I had to go to the very place where all these creepy creatures came from, and I had to find the queen of the whole damn bunch of them, who was sure to be the creepiest of all. And then I somehow had to sneak my way into her royal palace, or lair, or whatever it was, probably by making my way past a wall of fire or a horde of fire-breathing dragons. And after all that, I had to sweet-talk Her Strange Majesty into letting me have Andrea back and handing over that ointment.

But hell, why not? The next day wasn't a school day. I didn't have anything better to do.

By this time we'd reached the side of the store where they keep all the fruits and vegetables. I'd picked up a tomato, and I was squeezing it as if I knew the difference between a good one and a bad one, which I don't, and anyways in February in Winnipeg the only tomatoes we get are these hard square jobbies that it would take Arnold Schwarzenegger to squeeze out of shape. I think they breed them especially to take the long trip up from Mexico or wherever. They're more like little pink cardboard boxes than tomatoes.

But everyone squeezes them anyway, maybe to fool themselves into believing they really are tomatoes, and who am I to be different? The idea was to blend into the crowd, right?

So I was standing there lost in my thoughts about Strangers with this tomato-shaped object in my hand, and all of a sudden I heard this shriek. *Another* shriek. I was so surprised by it that I actually squeezed hard enough to split the tomato.

That's like cracking a bowling ball with your bare hands. Call me Mr. Universe.

"Liam, you jerk," I said furiously as I turned toward the noise, tomato juice dripping from my closed fist. "Why can't you—"

He wasn't here. How could he scream if he wasn't there?

"Hold your fire, Nesbit," said a nervous high-pitched voice in my ear. "It wasn't me. I'm right here." I turned. It was Liam, all right, standing right behind me and shaking in his boots in terror. The scream hadn't come from him. Then who—?

"It was her," he said in a loud whisper, pointing in the direction the noise had come from. "Over there by the plants."

As I wiped my gooey hand on one of those plastic vegetable bags, I looked where he was pointing. There at the back where they have all these houseplants and awful dyed carnations and such, a woman with a startled expression was looking down at the plant she'd just dropped, which was now sitting lopsided in the middle of a pile of dirt on the floor.

A crowd immediately gathered around the woman. I was about to join it, to find out what had happened, but Liam held me back.

"Stay here," he whispered again. "It might be . . . well, it might not be safe for you there."

That sounded ominous. I stood back and listened.

The woman who screamed was telling everybody that as soon as she picked up the plant, she noticed something really strange about the person who was standing near her, and that's why she freaked and dropped the plant.

"He was hollow," she said.

Liam, who was still holding on to my arm, suddenly tightened his grip. His face had turned dead white.

Well, more sort of a greenish white. And he was shaking so much, he looked like he'd been captured by an invisible paint-mixing machine.

Meanwhile, the screaming woman was still talking. "He looked perfectly normal from the front," she was saying. "Just like you or me or anybody. And then he turned around and . . . and he had no back."

It seemed he was like those masks you get for Halloween, the ones that are hollow in back so you can put your face in them. Except this guy was like a mask all over. A full body mask, with no body inside.

"It was awful," she said. "Awful." And as she thought about it, she made another little shriek.

Well, some of the people who'd gathered around tried to comfort her, and others started to pretend to look for this hollow guy, just to humor her. But in between her gasping and shrieking, the lady let us all know that he wasn't there anymore. He had disappeared as soon as she shrieked the first time. Just vanished.

And thinking about that made her shriek again.

Well, she finally pulled herself together and stopped shrieking and headed off toward the front of the store with this dazed expression on her face. And everyone else made little tut-tut speeches to each other about emotional exhaustion and mental breakdown and such, and went back to their shopping.

"Let me guess," I said to Liam. "It was one of them, right?"

"Of course it was one of them," he said in a low voice. "But we have to make sure. Come over here."

He grabbed our overloaded cart and wheeled it over to where that woman had been standing when she'd been screaming. I followed. By this time, one of the Safeway guys had got a broom and a dustpan and cleaned up the mess from the plant she'd dropped. But there was still a whole table of other plants sitting there.

The sign over the table said the plants were shamrocks, special for St. Patrick's Day.

Some joke. St. Patrick's Day was more than a month away, and they wanted us to start celebrating it already—by buying things, of course. And okay, I don't really know what a shamrock looks like, but to me these plants had a suspiciously close resemblance to the stuff we have growing in the front yard all summer for free.

Clover. And it was on special for $5.98 a pot. What a ripoff.

"Do what I do," Liam whispered urgently. He picked up one of the plants and stared out over the produce section.

I didn't get it, but it seemed harmless enough. I picked up the "shamrock" plant he pointed out to me and looked around, too.

It seemed to be just your usual Safeway crowd. Lots of women ignoring their screaming kids as they picked out carrots and lettuce, a few Yuppie-type guys with their hair greased back checking out the mangoes and persimmons.

"There," said Liam through clenched teeth. And he nudged my arm with his shoulder.

I looked in the direction he was pointing. It

was one of the Yuppie types, and he was weighing some vegetables. But he was—well, he was not quite himself.

He was hollow. I was looking at a hollow guy in half an overcoat. The front half. There was no back half at all. He looked like a Jell-O mold.

I suppressed a scream of my own and just stared. The hollow man looked up and caught us looking at him, and he smiled. He obviously didn't know we could see that he was hollow. And when I followed Liam's instructions and put the plant down again, I *couldn't* see that he was hollow. He was just an ordinary guy in an expensive overcoat and greasy hair.

Well, I didn't bother to get closer and check out his nostrils. I had this strong feeling I knew what I'd see anyway.

Oh, and by the way—the vegetables he was weighing? Guess what?

They were green beans.

Ten

"The world is in danger," Liam said in a squeaky voice, again looking nervously up at the darkening sky as we walked back from Safeway in the twilight.

He had insisted that we get out of the store immediately, as soon as we'd seen that hollow guy. "If he finds out we know about him," he said, "they'll all be on us, like flies on raw meat."

The mention of raw meat in that particular context had been a powerful persuader. We were already out of the store and across the crosswalk before I had a chance to ask Liam how come we could see that guy was hollow.

He told me as we headed down Osborne. It was because of those so-called shamrocks. They had to actually be clovers, just as I thought. And some of the plants must have been four-leaf clovers, because it seems we humans are able to see through the fairies' disguises when we're holding a four-leaf clover.

"Clovers have always been protection against Strangers," Liam said. "That's why people nowadays think that four-leaf clovers are lucky, even people who've never even heard of Strangers."

Well, lucky for everyone but the poor suckers who think they're buying shamrocks.

Anyway, our meeting with the hollow guy had convinced Liam that something had to be done, and fast. Before things got really bad.

As if my day hadn't been bad already.

"Yes," he said, looking upset again. "We really are going to have to do it. We're going to have to go there."

We? *We* have to go there?

"You're going to come with me?"

"Yes," he said in a surprisingly unhappy voice. "I have to. Mr. Rhymer says so."

"Why?" I said. I honestly couldn't think of a reason. I mean, it wasn't *his* sister they'd captured.

"Because I'm from there," he mumbled, so low I could hardly hear him. "Because I used to be one of them. I'm not now, of course. Not anymore. But Mr. Rhymer thinks if I go back, I'll start to remember. I'll remember their ways, and I'll be able to . . ." All of a sudden he was whining again. "I told him I probably wouldn't remember. I told him I'm a human now. I belong here, not there. I don't want to go back. I don't want to remember their ways. I hate their ways! But," he continued, his voice suddenly small again, "he said the whole human world depended on me. And if I really am a human now, then I should be willing to suffer a little to save my world, shouldn't I?"

He looked into my face and gave me this urgent look, desperate for me to agree with him. I nodded.

"That's what I thought," he said. "It's what a human would do for sure. So I'll do it, too. I'll go. I'll remember their stupid ways whether I want to or not. I'll help you find your sister. I'll act like I'm a stupid Stranger, and prove that I'm human once and for all."

We'd decided to do it that very night. I was going to sneak out of the house after everyone had gone to bed. That was the most dangerous part, Liam said. He didn't mean what my mom would do if she caught me. He meant being out at night when the Sky Yelpers would be thinking about a little bedtime snack.

Anyway, I'd sneak out and Liam would be waiting for me at the door to Stranger country. That was the sewer outlet he'd come through when he first got here. I would meet him there, and he and I would go through the door. Together.

A team of intrepid explorers, like Radisson and Groseilliers. Like Lewis and Clark.

Like Bert and Ernie.

And then the two of us would find the queen, and get the ointment, and rescue the baby, and close the door, and save the world from all these Strangers on the loose, wreaking havoc and stealing people's allowances and baby sisters.

And then we'd have breakfast.

Well, before I totally committed myself to this harebrained scheme, I decided I needed some proof. I needed something to persuade me that Liam wasn't just stringing me a line. Something to prove once and for all that that thing in the crib really wasn't Andrea.

So when I got home and I saw the coast was clear, I decided to try that business with the eggshells that Liam had told me about. Sure, it sounded dumb. But then, having a lazy fairy for a sister sounded dumb, too.

Mom was conveniently having a nap, and there were eggs in the fridge. I snuck the baby, or whatever it was, out of her crib and into the kitchen and plonked her down in this special large-economy-size baby seat we had to get for her—it was sitting in its usual spot on the counter, a few feet away from the stove, where Mom could keep an eye on her as she worked. She lay there like her usual lump, staring up at the ceiling, as I broke some eggs and threw away the insides. Then I tried to boil water in the shells.

My first discovery was that it isn't easy to boil water in eggshells on an electric stove. The eggs wouldn't stay straight, the water kept spilling, the shells scorched, and the baby just stared at me the same as always, although for a brief moment I thought I caught this just-exactly-who-do-you-think-you're-kidding? look on her face.

Then I had another idea. Mom was still asleep. Luckily the fire I'd started wasn't a very big one, and I'd managed not to scream too much while I was getting the burns. I still had some time.

So I left the kid sitting there in the kitchen and made a big production out of going out. I put on my ski jacket and hat and all, then firmly closed the door behind me. And then I quietly climbed up over a snowbank to the kitchen window and peeked inside, and watched to see what Andrea would do.

It took some time, enough to get me worried. The kid was just sitting there in her chair in the middle of an empty kitchen, and meanwhile I was freezing my buns off outside. What if Mom suddenly woke up from her nap and found the baby alone in the kitchen? I'd be dead meat.

Dead meat. I looked up anxiously at what turned out to be a blissfully empty sky and tried not to think about being meat as I crouched there and shivered. So this was how roasts felt in the freezer.

Finally, it happened.

The baby suddenly poked up her head. She actually moved—Andrea moved! Her cute little head looked this way and that all around the kitchen.

She soon decided the coast was clear—I was hidden behind the curtain, so she couldn't see me through the window. And she made this evil-looking smile.

Andrea smiled.

Then she climbed out of the baby chair, plopped herself down on the floor, marched across to the fridge, opened the door, and helped herself to one of my dad's beers.

I kid you not. A beer.

Not only did she take a beer, she stuck the bottle in between her delicate little baby gums and pulled the top off. And then she put her head back and swilled the beer down, all in one go.

Well, this was too much. Too much altogether. I blew my cover. I clambered off the snowbank, rushed back into the house and said, "Okay, buddy, your game's up, whoever you are. You're not Andrea and I know it."

She turned and looked at me calmly through her baby-blue eyes and said, "Big deal. What do you think you're going to do about it?"

I was so angry I didn't even have time to be flabbergasted that she was talking to me. *And* using big words.

"I'll . . . I'll tell them, I'll—" And I realized the Stranger was right. Nobody was going to believe that Andrea could even smile, let alone swill down a beer. Mom had already had one tantrum when I even just barely suggested the possibility of a Changeling.

"So talk all you want to, big boy," said this weird creature who still looked sort of like Andrea. "Talk away. And meanwhile, I'll just be lying there peacefully in that crib, and they'll end up carting *you* off to the booby hatch."

With which the disgusting little creep climbed back up onto the counter—it opened the doors and used the cupboard shelves as steps—and plomped itself down in the infant seat, and turned back into an unmoving nothing again.

And I was stuck with an empty beer bottle that I had to get rid of or else my parents would think it was me who drank it, which would be grounds for murder.

I was stuck with an empty beer bottle and a burning desire to head off to Stranger country immediately. I had a strong and pressing need for fairy ointment.

Eleven

As I quietly opened the back door that night, willing my parents not to hear me, the howling outside got louder and louder. The Yelpers were out in force, and they seemed to be awfully close. The noise seemed to be coming from right over my head. I shivered in my high-tops, standing there in the dark and the cold by the back door, unable to make my feet move.

Then, off in the distance, I heard what sounded like a horn. Not like the screech that kid made on the horn in the park. More like music. A wailing horn sound coming up under the yelps and howls.

The Yelpers must have heard it, too, because they were suddenly quiet, as if they were listening. Then, just as suddenly, their yelping began again, but now they were moving off, moving away from me. They seemed to be following the horn music, tracking it down.

Good.

I crossed my fingers for the poor slob blowing the horn, and I headed out of the yard and down the street in the dark of the night. With that music playing, it was like some dumb detective movie, with me as the star.

Or maybe a horror movie. With me as the dead meat.

It was pitch black out, the sky moonless and cloudy. I ran, getting more and more terrified. I ran faster and faster, down Fisher, down Churchill Drive, stumbling helter-skelter through the snow. And as I ran, I heard those howls off in the distance. By the time I'd made it under the bridge and all the way down the Drive to the pumphouse, I was panting like crazy.

But there was no time to rest, at least not while I was so obviously in view in the bright light from the lamppost there. I gulped some air and headed off the road into the deeper snow and safer darkness of the park.

It was only after I hurtled down the last steep part of the bank and out onto the flat of the frozen river that I finally saw some light again, a small circle of it. It was a flashlight. Cautiously, I went toward it.

The circle of light suddenly started to shake around violently, and an equally shaky voice came from behind it. "Nesbit? Is that you?"

It was Liam's voice. I'd recognize that quivering anywhere.

"Yes," I told him.

"Then it worked," he said a bit more calmly, the light still dancing around a little in his hand.

"What worked?"

"The music," he said proudly. "See, what I did was, I put all this horn music on a tape recorder. Wynton Marsalis."

Jazz. So that's what the Yelpers had headed off after. I wondered what Wynton would think about these formerly human cannibal-type dog monsters going for his music in such a big way.

"I set the tape recorder for the highest volume," Liam went on. "And then I hid it down in the bushes at the other end of the park, with a timer set to go off just when I arranged to meet you. I was hoping they'd think it was the horn of the Hunter, or at least be confused enough to go off and investigate. Which would put them as far as possible from us, see?"

He paused and smiled as he realized that the music was still playing, way off in the distance. "That's a good little recorder," he went on. "Top-notch human technology. It'll keep playing until the Yelpers destroy it. Or until someone calls the police about the loud noise. That should give us just enough time."

"Boy," I said, impressed, "you sure do know all about these Stranger things."

"It has nothing to do with Strangers," he said hotly. "I got the idea from *MacGyver* reruns on TV. *Human* TV."

"Oh," I said, then quickly changed the subject. "Have you found the door yet?"

He had. The sewer outlet was right behind him.

As he shone the flashlight onto it, I could see that it was nearly buried in snow. Only a small part of the metal grill was sticking out.

The two of us went to work, quickly clearing away as much snow as we could. Then we started to tug on the bars of metal that went across the opening.

They wouldn't budge.

The beam of Liam's flashlight showed why. The bars were bolted to a metal frame embedded in the concrete.

By now yelps were coming out of the sky again, and getting louder by the second. The Yelpers had obviously figured out the tape recorder. They didn't sound happy, and they seemed to be coming in our direction.

"Humph," said Liam. "I thought this might happen. It wasn't likely to be just lying open the way it was when I arrived here—not unless they actually *wanted* us to go through." He shrugged and put his hands in his pockets.

I was furious with him. Was he just going to quit so easily?

Then one of his hands came out of one of the pockets with a Vise-Grip in it. The other came out of the other pocket with a little acetylene torch.

"That's why I brought these along," he added. "Here, you take the torch and heat the bolts up a little. Just enough to get the ice out of them."

Then he calmly leaned over and began to undo the bolts. Maybe there was more to him than I'd thought.

As we worked, Liam chattered happily.

"This is a good tool," he said. "Good practical craftsmanship. I bet you don't find sensible tools like this in Stranger country. Hell, they probably don't even have a Canadian Tire there."

There were a lot of bolts—twelve on each side of the grill, twenty-four in all. Liam hummed Wynton Marsalis as he worked, following me and the torch down one side of the grill and then up the other, patiently undoing the bolts, apparently unconscious of the ever-louder yelping from the sky above us. I urged him to hurry.

"Slow and steady wins the race," he said, maddeningly calm as he undid bolt after bolt at a methodical pace.

Finally the job was finished. Liam put the Vise-Grip and torch back in his pockets, and we tried to lift up the grill.

Nothing happened. It was one heavy mother, that grill, and the opening it sat on was at a forty-five-degree angle. There was no way we had the strength to lift it off. We decided instead just to work at pushing it off to the side a little.

That we could do—although just barely. We

shoved and heaved for a long time, and finally the door was open, open just enough for us to squeeze through.

Meanwhile, the barking in the sky was getting louder. And I remembered once more how good I was supposed to smell to them.

"We've got no more time to lose," I said. "Let's go, Liam. Now." I picked up the flashlight he'd dropped on the snow and began to head past the grill and into the hole.

But Liam didn't come. When I looked back to find out what had happened to him, I could see him still just standing there on the river outside the sewer.

I turned on the flashlight and pointed it toward him. He didn't even blink—just kept on standing there, staring into the light in this unseeing way, shivering.

"I can't," he finally said in this really low voice. "I just can't. I can't and I won't."

I didn't know what to do. The noise in the sky was getting louder and louder, closer and closer. But Liam didn't even seem to hear it. I couldn't just run down the sewer and leave him there, could I? No, I should move my butt out there and help him. Out of my safe hiding hole, out into full view of the open sky and the . . . and them.

As I stood there trying to make up my mind, Liam suddenly shook all over, as if coming awake out of a trance. Then he did blink, and his eyes glared accusingly into the beam of light.

"No!" he shouted. "I won't. It's *your* problem, Nesbit, not mine. It's your sister and it's your problem. I don't care what Mr. Rhymer says. I'm a human now. I wouldn't remember their ways, I know I wouldn't. I don't *want* to remember their ways. I belong here, not there."

"But . . ." I couldn't think what to say. But whatever it was, I had to say it fast. The howls weren't very far away at all. Even if Liam didn't want to come, I had to get him into the sewer, where it was safer. "But it's not just my sister, Green," I finally got out. "It's the world, it's—"

"The world!" he shouted. "Some joke, Nesbit! The human world! *My* world! But the only way I get to save it is to go there and stop being human. And then it wouldn't be my world anymore, would it? I can only save it by giving it up. So I guess the joke's on me, eh? On little old Liam Green, on—"

Then his words stopped being words and turned into a strange garbled noise. A sort of a shriek, another masterpiece from the King of Screams. But this one was different. It sounded crazy, uncontrolled. Like he'd totally lost his senses. Like he was screaming and laughing at the same time.

Then, that noise still pouring out of his mouth, he turned and strode off into the snow, walking down the river just as he had that first day when he'd come out of this very same sewer.

"Liam!" I screamed. "Come back; it's too dangerous. The Yelpers, remember the Yelpers. You can't just—"

But he could, and he did.

He disappeared into the darkness.

Me, I just stood there staring at his back as he stalked off, furious with him once more. It's a good thing he isn't coming, I thought. Fat lot of use he'd be, the cowardly little creep.

And he was just going to have to look out for himself. The howling in the sky was still there, and by now it was almost directly overhead. I had my own butt to save, and fast. As quickly as I could, I put the flashlight into my pocket and then started to tug on the grate to close the hole again. It was heavy, that grate, really heavy. I was hardly able to move it. But somehow, finally, I got the hole covered. I was safe.

I just stood there looking out through the grate, panting in exhaustion, and listened to a sky full of yelping.

And then, from not very far off in the darkness in front of me, there was a scream—a loud, high-pitched scream mixing in with the yelps.

And then, abruptly, silence.

No more barking.

No more scream.

Nothing.

It was the most frightening silence I had ever heard.

Twelve

I stood there, looking out at darkness and listening to nothing, trying not to think what I was thinking. Liam.

No, it couldn't be. He had to be far away from here by the time that scream came.

He had to be.

And anyway, I remembered, didn't the Yelpers have to hear the horn blow before they attacked? And the horn hadn't blown, so they couldn't have—

"They'd think it was the horn of the Hunter." It was Liam's voice I was hearing inside my head, proudly telling me about his tape recorder. And maybe his trick had worked—worked too well. They were just dumb dogs, after all. They probably wouldn't know the difference between Wynton Marsalis and a bicycle bell, let alone the horn of the Hunter. So maybe the Yelpers did think they'd heard the Hunter's horn, and then they came after the first warm body they could find, and—

And did what they did.

But still, Liam was smart. He'd hide. It was probably just a dog. They *liked* dogs. Yeah, Liam was probably halfway home by now, thinking up a good story to tell that Mr. Rhymer about why he hadn't come with me.

But you know, the more I told myself it wasn't him, the less convinced I felt. That scream hadn't sounded like any dog. What else could it have been but someone out alone in the dark night?

Someone with a habit of screaming.

Someone, I realized with a sinking feeling, who probably had my scent on him.

The words "dead meat" entered my mind yet again. I didn't want to think about that. And I didn't want to think about Liam anymore either.

So I made myself stop looking out into that empty, silent darkness. I made myself turn around, and I reached into my pocket for the flashlight, and I shone the light down into the darkness of the tunnel. And I started to follow on after it.

At first it was just ice and snow and blackness. But as I walked, the ice began to have puddles of water on it, and I felt myself getting warmer.

Soon I was slogging through water. The bottoms of my jeans got soaked, and as for my shoes, well, I was glad my mom wasn't there to say "I told you so." Not that I couldn't hear her saying it in my mind anyway: "I told you those hightops weren't enough for winter. I told you at least a hundred times. What's wrong with good solid boots, I'd like to know."

I wasn't exactly walking in the most pleasant-smelling water either. This was a sewer outlet, after all. Given the smell, I was seriously beginning to wonder if it was anything *but* a sewer outlet. It sure didn't smell like any fairyland.

Eventually, thank goodness, the smell began to fade. Soon it was just like fresh water, like a stream in the country.

And the cleaner it got and the less it smelled like a sewer, the more edgy I found myself getting.

I mean, walking around in a sewer is no picnic. But except for the bad smell and the interesting squishy lumps you sometimes feel under your feet, the worst thing you might expect there is rats, maybe.

But now it wasn't a sewer anymore. It was more like a cave or a tunnel, with walls of earth and rocks and the occasional root sticking out of the roof. It was a dark place down under the earth that didn't smell anything like a toilet. I could imagine all sorts of interesting possibilities.

Evil dwarfs, for instance, lobbing rocks at me in order to protect their secret hoards of stolen gold. Man-eating trolls with two or three heads and two or three mouths and two or three sets of sharp teeth.

Hell, for all I knew I'd already walked right into the open jaws of a giant snake so huge it filled up the entire tunnel. I might be making my way right through its intestines at this very moment, and the liquid that occasionally dripped down on me from above might be snake digestive juices. Any minute I might start dissolving.

But I didn't. And as I slogged my way forward, I realized it was getting lighter. Light enough for me to see the outlines of three or four evil trolls on the path ahead of me.

After nearly jumping out of my skin, I realized they were just rocks. And I kept walking.

It was getting lighter and lighter all the time. I turned off the flashlight and stuck it in my pocket. Finally, I could see the end.Once I saw it, I stopped for a minute to pull myself together, steeling myself to step out into Stranger country.

So I'd made my way safely through the tunnel. No snake, no trolls, nothing. It made me really mad.

I mean, those damn Strangers had done it to me again. They always managed to do the opposite of what I expected.

I'd expected my allowance and I got a lecture from my mom. I'd expected Andrea and I got a beer-guzzling moron. I'd expected help from Liam and I got . . . well, I didn't get much help, did I?

And now I'd expected the worst and I got . . . nothing. Zilch. Zero.

I had no idea what I might find when I

stepped through the hole and left the tunnel. On the other side there might be Disneyland castles and giant Ferris wheels and dancing clowns. There might be evil giants and elves and dragons. Or there might be nothing—literally nothing—and I'd step off into a void and just fall through space forever.

But I'd come this far, and there was no way I was going back. So I closed my eyes and told myself to be brave and stepped out, expecting anything.

Anything but what I actually did see when I opened my eyes again.

I was standing at the mouth of a cave, looking out at a river almost directly below me. And I recognized the river. It was the Red. The river that goes by Churchill Drive Park. The river I'd just come from.

That's right, it was the same river. The banks, the trees, the river all looked the way they would have looked if I had still been standing by that sewer outlet.

But not quite the same way.

For one thing, it was summer. I'd walked through a tunnel from winter into summer. There was no ice, just murky brown water. The trees were covered with leaves. The banks were covered with grass and weeds.

Another thing: the sky was green instead of blue—a deep green. And the light was dim, like it sometimes gets in twilight.

And there were no houses on the opposite bank—just trees and that green sky.

No houses. And when I scrambled up the

bank and took a look around, there was no pump-house and no Churchill Drive.

No houses. No road. No streetlamps. Except for that weird green sky, it looked the way it must have looked centuries ago, before people came to Canada from Europe and built Winnipeg.

It was the same place, all right. But it wasn't the same place at all. It was different. Totally different.

Thirteen

"So now what?" I said to myself as I took off my ski jacket and stared in bewilderment at this leafy and very green place that looked unsettlingly like it ought to have been Churchill Drive.

In one way, at least, I was glad it wasn't Churchill Drive, because if it had been, where I was standing would have been right in the middle of the pumphouse, with all those pumps and things grinding away at my tender bod. Talk about your dead meat—your dead hamburger meat.

But there was no pumphouse. I'd come to the country of the Strangers. The queen was here, somewhere, and so was that ointment I was supposed to get. And Andrea.

But that was the problem. Where, exactly? I mean, I didn't really expect a yellow brick road or anything. But jeez, you'd think the local tourist bureau might at least have been kind enough to put up a sign: "This Way to the Ointment and the Stolen Sister."

But there was no sign. There probably wasn't even any tourist bureau. And there sure as hell wasn't any yellow brick road or, for that matter, any road at all. Except for that funny green sky, it was just an ordinary place on a quiet riverbank.

As I stood there looking around and trying to decide what to do, I began to feel this light breeze tickling my neck. At first I hardly noticed it. It was gentle, delicate. It felt . . . well, to tell the truth, it felt really good. I was enjoying it before I even realized it was happening.

Then I heard a little giggle. It was no wind. There was someone there behind me. I blushed and turned around to see who was making me feel so great.

There was a girl standing there behind me, a really great-looking girl with long flowing black hair and big blue eyes. Oh, and one other thing. Except for that hair, she was naked. Stark naked. This gorgeous naked girl had been breathing on my neck, and she was looking at me as if I was the best thing she'd ever seen in her whole life.

"Hi, John," she said in a warm voice. "Lovely day, isn't it?" Without even thinking about how she knew my name, I dropped my jacket and reached out for her.

And please don't ask me how come I did that. I mean, I wouldn't lunge at any other girl like that, not without at least asking permission first. But this girl was different. She was the girl of my dreams—some of my more embarrassing dreams. She was mine, all mine, and somehow I just knew that she wouldn't be the least bit upset by my acting like some dumb-ass jock on steroids.

So I did. There I was grabbing for her like a depraved sex maniac, and poof! She was gone. She just suddenly disappeared altogether.

Well, I guess that should have been a clue, right? I should have realized something was not quite right. But before I could even think about it, I heard another giggle, and there she was again. Standing about twenty meters away, though, down by the slope of the riverbank, with her long black hair streaming out around her naked body. And she was calling. Calling my name.

Still not thinking about it, I leaped up and ran to her. And again, as soon as I got there, she wasn't there anymore. Now she was closer to the river, just by the edge. I leaped up and after her once more.

But by now she was in the river itself. Right in the middle of the river, floating with her hair spread out around her and calling, still calling my name.

It was dumb, but I couldn't stop myself. I jumped in after her, clothes and all. Jumped in and swam toward her and grabbed her. I held on to her, wildly excited, and I nestled my head into her long black hair. It smelled sweet, perfumey—and something else, something hard to describe. What was that smell? I opened my eyes and looked at the hair I was snuggling into.

Weeds. There were water weeds growing in it, mingled with the beautiful long black hair. Water weeds like the algae that grows in lakes and rivers in the summer. I'd been smelling algae. I pulled my head back, shocked.

As I looked at her, bewildered, she suddenly gave me this big fat smile. This very nasty smile.

The nastiest thing about it was, I could see that her teeth were bright fluorescent green, and pointed. Bright-green pointy teeth in the middle of that beautiful face of my dreams.

She smiled. And then she began to cackle madly.

Guess what? I suddenly wasn't excited anymore. I was just mad. I pushed her off me. I went under and nearly drowned. Finally I managed to make it back to the shore, sputtering and spewing water.

As I sat there coughing up water and feeling wet and stupid, the girl floated in the middle of the river, her long black hair spread out around her on the surface of the water, flashing her green teeth at me and cackling away madly.

"What's wrong, John Nesbit?" she called out. "You don't find old Jenny Greenteeth so attractive after all? Poor little Johnny. That'll teach you to look before you leap." Then she cackled again and dove under the water, and was gone.

Ho-ho. Some funny joke. So funny I forgot to laugh.

I was furious, but with myself more than with her. I mean, I figured I'd got what I deserved for behaving in that dumb-ass jock way. Even if she had enchanted me somehow so that I couldn't help myself, I still felt like a king-size dork. I resolved to be more on my guard.

Anyway, I was sopping wet, and the only thing I could think of to dry myself off with was my ski jacket. Well, Mom would kill me if she ever found out, but I had no choice—the water smelled like disgusting algae. I picked the jacket up from the ground where I'd dropped it before, and started wiping my face and hair.

As I sat there wiping and trying to decide what to do next, I heard a noise. It sounded like bells, and also this regular pounding sound, like drums maybe. Or like someone hitting the ground. It was coming from somewhere off to my left.

I turned toward it. Away off in the distance, just about where the bridge and the Monkey Paths would be back in Riverview, I could see a group of people. People or something else—it was too far away to tell. Whatever it was, it was a group of them, and they were coming toward me.

I got back up onto my feet and looked around wildly for someplace to hide. There wasn't any. It was too late for me to make it back to the cave, and I certainly wasn't about to jump into the river and try to swim for it, not with that living advertisement for orthodontia floating around under the surface. They, whatever they were, were coming fast, and there was no way to escape from them.

As I stood there in a panic, watching who knows what get closer and closer to me, they disappeared. Blinked out, like Jenny Greenteeth had. But not exactly like Jenny had, because I could still hear the jingling and the pounding, louder and louder all the time. I just couldn't see anything.

Before I even realized what I was doing, I found myself scrambling up the bank, going toward the sound instead of away from it. I don't know why my curiosity triumphed over my good sense. Maybe it was another spell.

At the top, there was a grassy place like a lawn. I could see a big circle of mushrooms growing in it, like those ones you find in the park back home after it's rained a lot.

My mom once told me those mushroom circles are called Fairy Rings. And maybe that has something to do with what happened next, because as I listened to that sound get closer and closer, I felt myself pulled toward that circle of mushrooms. Soon I was standing inside the circle, surrounded by mushrooms.

And as I stood there under a sky full of bells and pounding sounds, looking down thoughtlessly at one of the mushrooms and wondering why I'd made myself go there, something suddenly appeared beside the mushroom.

A hoof. It looked like a horse's hoof.

It was a horse's hoof. And now there was a horse attached to it. And then there were a whole bunch of horses.

The pounding I'd been hearing was the horses'

hooves. The jingling sound was bells on their harnesses. And they stopped being invisible as soon as they crossed that ring of mushrooms.

Horses. Just ordinary horses circling around me.

Horses and, I could see as I looked up, ordinary riders.

Well, more or less ordinary. I mean, they looked like fully grown adults with beards and all, but they were no larger than little kids. Come to think of it, they looked sort of like the Seven Dwarfs in *Snow White*.

By this time the horses and riders were circling me, the bells jingling madly. As I turned to follow them riding around me, I lost my footing and put my hand against one of the horses to steady myself.

As soon as I touched its mane, the horse began to move more quickly. I didn't let go, because I was afraid I'd fall. The horse kept right on moving, and I found myself being pulled along, running beside the horse, circling. And then I was even more afraid to let go. I thought I might get trampled by the other horses, which by now were galloping right along behind us.

Meanwhile, my horse was gaining speed. I was holding on for dear life. I was . . . I was being pulled through the air. My feet were totally off the ground, and the ground was falling farther and farther below me. I could see the circle of mushrooms far below me.

I was flying.

Now for sure I was not going to let go.

As I desperately clutched that poor horse's mane and flew through the air, the rider looked down at me and said calmly, "So it's a ride you'll be wanting, is it, young human? There's no sense hanging there like that. Too windy by half. Hop on, hop on."

"Gee, thanks, mister," I said as clearly and politely as I could, considering the fact that I was being hurtled along at an enormous speed and that my teeth were gritted together out of sheer terror. But my mom had taught me always to be polite. "I wish I could, believe me. But I can't, there's no room."

It was true. The rider filled the saddle on the back of the horse, and there was nowhere else to sit.

"Of course there is," he said. "See?"

I looked. Before my eyes, the horse sort of stretched and grew longer, its front legs and back legs growing farther apart from each other. And the saddle grew longer with it. Handy, eh? The Amazing Expand-a-Horse, for your growing family's needs. Now there was room enough for two.

Somehow I twisted around and grabbed onto the rider's arm, still being pulled through the air, and then managed to slide myself up onto the horse and into the seat that was now awaiting me.

As soon as I was seated, I heard the driver's bored voice saying, "And where might you be wanting to go, human?" He sounded like a cab driver—as if this was the way people usually hailed a cab in this place.

"Come now, human," he added impatiently. "You were standing in that ring. You must want to go somewhere. So where?"

I'd been standing in that ring. So that *was* the way you hailed a cab here. I suddenly relaxed. I mean, it wasn't a kidnapping or anything, just a Stranger taxi service. And this flying business wasn't so bad once you got used to it. Better than a Winnipeg Transit bus. Less stuffy, and cheaper, too. Fun.

"Look, human," the rider said curtly, interrupting my pleasant thoughts. "I haven't got all day. Tell me where you want to go, or I'll dump you."

Dump me? I looked down to the ground below.

Way, way down.

Not your usual view from a bus window. Suddenly I remembered why I was here in the first place. Andrea. The ointment.

"To the queen," I said. "I want to go to the Stranger queen's castle."

"The castle, is it? Well, human, it's your life." And before I could ask him what he meant, he shouted, "Ho and away, boys, for the royal castle!" And off we all went, so fast that the ground far beneath us was almost a blur.

We flew in silence—except for the bells, of course, and the horses' panting, and that wind. As I looked down through it, I could see we were flying rapidly inland from the riverbank, heading what would have been north if we'd still been back home. The country below seemed to be laid out in little squares, with the trees mostly near the edges of the squares, and the squares all lined up against long narrow stretches of bare land. It was just like lawns and streets, except there weren't any houses in the middle of the lawns or streets running over the bare parts.

It was exactly the way Winnipeg would look if you took away all the houses and the people and the other artificial things people had made, but left behind the natural things people had planted there.

Somehow that was creepier than if there'd been no lawns and no trees planted in regular patterns. It was so much like home—and so different.

We crossed another river, about where the Assiniboine was back home. Then ahead and a little off to my left, I finally saw a building.

A building that looked like a castle. Three towers with pointy roofs, each tower on one of the castle's corners. Stone walls. A moat filled with water going around the whole thing. And a bridge on chains going over the moat in front of a big arched doorway.

It looked familiar, that building. Very familiar. But I couldn't think why. I mean, where would I have ever seen a building like that, except maybe in some stupid Disney fairy-tale movie?

A fairy-tale castle. How appropriate. I was heading for a fairy-tale castle with the Seven Dwarfs, and the queen was probably inside in her witch laboratory, busy fixing up a poisoned apple to offer me.

Anyway, me and the dwarfs finally came down just in front of the big arched door on the lawn by the end of the bridge.

As soon as the horse's hooves hit the ground,

I felt this really weird sensation under my butt. Like a gigantic joy buzzer. It was the horse and the saddle snapping back to their former size. Zip, and there was nothing left for me to sit on but air, and so there I was, sitting on air, and sliding over the back end of the horse and down onto the ground.

Oof. As soon as my butt stopped tingling and I got my wind back, I opened my eyes and stood up to thank the rider for the lift. I mean, I didn't think all that much of the landing procedure, but what did you want for free?

I was too late. They were gone. Totally gone. I turned wildly in all directions, but I couldn't see anybody.

They'd taken off as quickly as they'd come. I was alone again. A stranger in Stranger land, with no one to help me or guide me. What should I do?

Well, there was only one thing *to* do.

My sister Andrea might be inside that castle.

Fourteen

I stepped through the door of the castle into a room so big that it seemed to take up all the space inside the building, from the front to the back and from the floor right up to the roof. High over my head the ceiling glinted and gleamed. It looked like the whole thing was made of diamonds.

But despite the ceiling there was almost no light in that huge room, only torches burning in brackets on the walls, and with just those bits of light glinting here and there in the darkness, it took a while for my eyes to adjust. Meanwhile, I listened to what sounded like a really wild party. Music playing. Laughing and shouting.

Eventually I could see it *was* a wild party. There was a band playing this really horrible music—

tambourines and violins and even an accordion. It sounded like a demented version of that gross Irish music they try to get you to buy on TV. The stuff that's not available in stores, for obvious reasons. Who'd actually want to buy it?

But people were dancing to the band anyway, and they seemed to be having a fine old time. They were people of all sizes—or, I guess, not people, but Strangers.

Some did look just like ordinary people. Some looked like ordinary people with green skin. But some were very small and very cute, like those guys on the horses. And off in one corner there was a giant dancing all by himself while he swigged wine from a huge bottle. He must have been two stories tall, and everybody else was keeping well out of his way, which seemed wise. He was really wasted. If one of his giant feet happened to land on you while you were dancing, I bet you'd immediately look like a swatted mosquito.

The giant, at least, looked like a person. A large fat drunk person, but a person. A lot of the others didn't look like people at all. As my eyes adjusted to the darkness of the room, I could see little dragons talking with dwarfs, things that looked sort of like flames in the shape of human bodies floating around dancing skeletons, empty suits of armor dancing with their arms around what looked like beautiful long dresses with nobody inside them. It was an unusual group.

Down at the other end of the room, past that weird crowd and beyond the murky darkness, I could make out a huge fire burning in a hearth, and in front of it, some people sitting at a long table on this raised platform. That was probably where the queen was.

So I steeled myself and headed into the crowd, pushing my way past all these people with horse heads and horses with human heads. As I steered my way around this character holding a wineglass and alternately sipping from it first with the mouth in one of its heads and then with the mouth in the other, somebody danced right into my back and nearly pushed me over.

"Hey, creep," I heard this surly but sort of familiar voice say, "just where do you think you're going anyway? I'd like to—Nesbit! It's you."

I turned to look at who'd bumped me, astonished that somebody else in that weird place knew my name. I was even more astonished when I saw who it was. It was my buddy Mark, hanging on to a girl.

Mark. A kind of wasted Mark—I could smell the beer on his breath. The turkey had been into his father's party supplies again.

"Hey, Rob," he said, shouting over his shoulder. "Look who's here!" And then he turned back to me. "Why didn't you say you were coming, John? We coulda come together."

"Come? Together? Here?" I was confused. What was *Mark* doing here anyway? Had he come down the sewer, too, or—

"And anyway," he added, standing there and

swaying a little, "what made you decide to come? I thought you didn't like these socials."

"Socials?" What was he talking about?

"Yeah," said Rob, who'd come up and was standing beside Mark with his arm around this other girl. They were a matched pair, those girls—dyed black hair and leather jackets and tube tops and miniskirts and black stockings. And big earrings and bigger nose rings. And lipstick out to their ears. Definitely not my type.

My type, I remembered with a sinking feeling, had green fangs. And thinking about those green fangs made me very wary of these girls.

As the girls gave me the once-over, Mark added, "You always say these community club dances suck."

I was even more confused. This was the country of the Strangers, for Pete's sake, the castle of the Stranger queen. It wasn't stupid old Riverview Community Center with people stomping on each other's toes and barfing in the john on a Friday night.

"Look," I said, reaching out and grabbing Mark's arm, "you guys are confused. You—"

As soon as I touched him, I wasn't in the castle anymore. I *was* in the community club. Just like Rob said.

I looked around, astonished. The bunch of us were standing in the community club, and it was dark, and there was a dance going on all around us. Just like in the castle, except the music was a lot tastier. And the monsters were a little less obvious. No dancing flames or two-headed babes. Just some skinhead types in steel-toed Doc Martens.

I was so shocked, I let go of Rob's arm and stared around me. No club. It was the castle again.

I touched him again.

The community club again.

So it was true. These guys *were* in the community club, just like they said. But they were here in the Stranger castle at the same time. And when I touched them, I was in the community club, too. How could it be?

"Listen, John, I got something to tell you." Mark leaned over so the girl he was with couldn't hear him, and he whispered, "Hey, man, check out these major babes we picked up. Good stuff, eh?"

Trying not to choke on the beer fumes that were pouring out of him, I took another glance at the girl pasted to him. This was his idea of major? Bodychecking must do something weird to the brain.

"As soon as I asked this one to dance, she grabbed onto me and she won't let go. She's hot, really hot, man. You want me to ask if they have a friend for you, too?" He gave a wink and poked me in the ribs.

Oh, sure. I could just see myself with that lipstick smeared all over my face. And wouldn't the nose ring get in the way?

And what if she had green teeth?

"No, thanks," I said. "I . . . I've got something I have to do."

Well, it was true, I did. I had to find the

queen. I had to ask for the ointment and get Andrea back.

And I had to figure out how these guys could be in two different places at the same time without even knowing it.

"Yeah, sure," Mark said. "You got something to do. Sure. Just scared is all." And he spun his so-called babe around and danced off, with Rob and his so-called babe following right behind them.

I stood there and watched those girls holding on to them for dear life as they danced in two different places at once. And I tried to figure it out.

There was only one possible explanation. The usual explanation. Those girls had to be Strangers—Strangers disguised as Rob and Mark's dorky idea of female perfection. Apparently, disguising yourself as some poor sucker's idea of female perfection was a local custom around here. And when Rob and Mark danced with those Strangers, they were caught up in Stranger life. That's why I could see them, why they could be in two places at once. Rob and Mark thought they were dancing at a plain old community club social. They didn't even know they were also at a party in another country.

If Strangers were involved, it had to be dangerous. And to tell the truth, those girls looked dangerous even if they were just plain human beings with ordinary human teeth. I rushed after Rob and Mark to warn them.

As I ran, I slipped on something on the floor and fell.

I looked at what I'd fallen in. Red liquid. A familiar-looking red liquid. I put my finger in it. It was sticky.

Blood.

Freaked, I sat there staring at the fresh blood. It formed a trail across the floor, and the trail led to Rob and Mark as they danced away from me in the arms of those so-called babes. The blood was dripping from Rob's and Mark's bodies.

It was their blood, oozing out of their shirts and dripping down onto the floor. Those girls were squeezing the blood out of them, squeezing the life out of them.

And all the time they thought they were just having fun at a social at the community club.

I had to stop them. With a roar, I rushed over and barreled myself into them.

For an amateur it was a pretty good body-check. I pushed all four of them over onto the floor.

As Rob and Mark separated from the girls, they blinked out of sight.

Good. They were back home again. And wondering, probably, where those so-called babes had gone. And where I had gone. And why they felt so weak all of a sudden.

Well, they'd probably put it down to the beer. And they'd be so furious with me, they'd either beat me up the next time they saw me or just cut me dead. I could look forward to a few days blissfully free of hockey discussions. If I ever got back home, that is.

Meanwhile, back in the castle, those two girls

just sat there in the middle of the Stranger party, calmly staring at me, and I just sat there staring back at them, waiting for them to try something.

"Hey, cutie," one of them finally said. She gave me a great big lipstick-laden smile that showed a large set of teeth—pearly white teeth, thank the Lord for small mercies. "How's about a dance?"

"No, me," said the other with an even bigger and even whiter smile. "How's about a dance with me?"

And they both reached out for me.

"No, thanks," I said firmly. "I . . . I think I'll just sit this one out."

"Your loss, human," one of them said indifferently. Then she started looking around, as if she were seeking out another victim.

"Those two drunk ones are gone," she said, "but there's another likely pair over there." Her friend looked to where she was pointing. So did I, but I couldn't see anyone.

Well, if they were looking for more victims, they had to be looking in the club, not here. And apparently they couldn't even see Rob and Mark there anymore. Probably gone home to sleep it off. Good.

As I watched, the girls shifted out of focus, sort of like static on a TV. When they came back into focus, they were two tough-looking hunks in leather jackets and tight jeans and greasy hair. Male hunks.

They were Strangers, all right.

"I'll take the blonde," one of them said in a

husky voice. Then they stood up, smirked like a couple of oversexed jocks, and strutted off through the crowd toward their prey.

I gazed after them, hoping they'd touch their victims and I'd see who it was. But I lost them in the darkness, and I never did get to see which girls they might be after.

I hoped it wasn't anyone I knew.

Meanwhile, I was still sitting there on the floor in the middle of the Stranger party, and nobody seemed to care. Nobody had even noticed when I'd bodychecked Rob and Mark and those girls. Apparently stuff like that happened here all the time. What a life.

I shrugged, picked myself up, and continued on my way toward that big fireplace.

Just before I got there, I heard someone calling my name—again.

"Johnny! Johnny Nesbit," the voice said. "You did it. You got here!"

I turned and looked at where the voice was coming from.

It was Mrs. F. Mrs. F., sitting behind a pillar in the same weird chair I'd seen in the park. Mrs. F., sitting there in the Stranger castle.

And she had my sister Andrea on her lap.

Andrea looked terrific. Rosy cheeks, lively eyes, healthy, smiling. And when she saw me, she reached out her arms toward me. It almost made me cry.

I reached back, smiling like crazy, and I was just about to take her from Mrs. F. and give her a big hug when I heard this loud voice behind me.

"Well," it said. "Fee-fi-fo-fum, to coin a phrase. And what have we here?"

"Oh," said Mrs. F., suddenly looking up and trembling. "Your majesty!" She quickly clambered out of her chair and bowed down low to the ground, nearly bumping the back of Andrea's head into the floor. As she bowed, she whispered to me, "Bow, Johnny! It's the queen! Bow, or we'll all be sorry."

So I bowed, and then looked up to see who I was bowing to.

She was a queen, all right—a classy woman who looked like she owned everything, and deserved to own it, and knew she deserved to own it. It was proud and arrogant, that look on her face.

"And who is this . . . this interloper in my castle?" she asked, looking down her nose at me as if I were a disgusting, puny bug.

"This," said Mrs. F. in a flattering and clearly frightened voice, "this is Johnny, your majesty. Johnny Nesbit. He's, well, he's Andrea's brother."

"Andrea's brother? Indeed! I thought I smelled human blood. And just what is Andrea's brother doing here?" She gave me this piercing stare.

I stared back, trying hard not to blink.

"I . . . I came to get my sister back," I said weakly. But I didn't blink. Pretty good, for a puny little bug.

The queen got a surprised look on her face.

"You have, have you? Well, we'll see about that. Meanwhile, though, it's time for dinner. Come, come. The banquet awaits!" She turned around and swept back toward the huge table that was sitting on that raised place in front of the fireplace.

As I moved to follow her, Mrs. F. grabbed my arm and whispered urgently at me, "Watch out, Johnny. Don't eat. Don't eat their—"

But before she could finish, the queen looked back over her shoulder and said, "You stay here, nurse-maid."

In terror, Mrs. F. slumped back into her chair. And me, I had no choice. I headed off after the queen.

Fifteen

So I was sitting there at a banquet table with a banquet going on, being offered all this food. Good food, too. Not the sort of high-class swill you'd expect at a banquet, but burgers and fries and pizza slices. And I was saying, "No, thanks, ma'am, I'm just not hungry today," to this bossy person who was getting angrier at me with every passing minute.

I felt like a real goof. But you know, when the queen pulled me over and sat me down in front of all that food, Mrs. F.'s words were still echoing in my mind. "Don't eat. Don't eat their—" Their what? Their burritos? I mean, there wasn't a poisoned apple in sight. Anyway, I wasn't going to take any chances. I just refused to eat everything.

It wasn't easy. I hadn't had anything since supper the night before. I was starving, and all these cheeseburgers and pepperoni pizzas and onion rings kept being passed before my eyes. And what was the big problem anyway? Was I going to get Montezuma's revenge, like people do when they travel to Mexico, and end up spending my time in Stranger country on the john? It took all my energy to keep saying "No, thank you, ma'am" again and again and again.

Finally the queen got really furious.

"Not hungry, eh?" she said, this wicked gleam in her eyes. "We'll see about that, human. Have this." She grabbed this big bean burrito and shoved it toward my mouth.

Some manners *she* had. The queen of England sure wasn't going to invite *her* to a garden party.

Well, she wasn't going to get away with it, and that was that. I clenched my teeth shut and held on for dear life as she ground the burrito into my face.

"Eat! Eat, you insignificant little twerp!" she shouted. By this time the music had stopped, and all the Strangers in the hall had stopped dancing and talking and were staring at us.

But I kept my teeth clenched, putting all my strength into it. I was mad now, and I was not going to give in. No way.

And so I didn't have to.

"I give up," the queen finally said, falling into her chair and dropping the mushed-up bits of burrito back onto the table. "You're too willful for me, human. You've won."

Won? Won what? I still didn't know *why* I wasn't supposed to eat the food.

But I was feeling pretty good anyway, because I was remembering what my mom always said. So my willfulness was going to get me into trouble someday, was it? And now I'd won something because of it. A lot my mom knew.

"And so," the queen went on, "I must grant you a boon, my willful young friend."

What was a boon?

"What do you wish, mortal?" the queen added.

Oh. A wish. Neat!

What did I wish? That was obvious. "Andrea," I said. "I want Andrea."

"No," she said, quickly, icily. "Anything but that, anything—riches, magical powers, anything. But not the child. She's mine. You can't have her."

"But I don't want anything else. I just want my sister back."

"You can't have her. Unless—" She paused. "No. It wouldn't be possible."

"What?" I said quickly. "*What* wouldn't be possible?"

"If a man had come, a great hero of humankind . . . But you're just a boy." She looked me up and down like a judge at a dog show inspecting a mongrel who'd got in by mistake. "A mere stripling. And yet," she added thoughtfully, "you have the will, certainly, the will to resist, the will to win. Perhaps . . . there just might be a chance."

"Anything," I said. "I'll do anything."

"Then perhaps it's worth a try. Of course," she said in a matter-of-fact way, "you do understand that the most likely result is your own painful death?"

I gulped. "Yes," I whispered, "if you say so."

"Good, good," she said calmly. "Now sit, and I'll explain it to you."

As she told me about it, she became less and less like a queen and more like just a sad person with a big problem. A really big problem.

"I must keep your sister," she said, "or I will lose my own life. That's why I arranged to take her in the first place, once I discovered the door was open. Why I took her and the nursemaid there"—she pointed over to where Mrs. F. was sitting with Andrea—"to feed her. It was the Hunter, you see. You know of him?"

"You mean the head honcho of the Yelpers?"

"Yes. The Hunter. When my consort left this country, I was alone here. Alone and defenseless. The Hunter took advantage of it. He drove his troops upon us, and then he forced himself upon me. He made me marry him, against my will. And will I had, my lad, let me assure you. Will I had, as strong as yours and stronger. For my heart was elsewhere."

"But why?" I said. "I don't understand why he wanted to marry you."

"Use your eyes," she said, a fiery look on her face.

Oops.

"No, no, I didn't mean that," I said quickly.

"And lucky for you that you didn't. From a

Stranger, such words would be grounds for instant execution." Considering the look she gave me when she thought I was insulting her, I could believe it.

"But you're right," she continued. "The Hunter didn't really care for me. It was the power he wanted. The Yelpers have always resented their position here in my country. He wanted only the power, and he took it, just as he takes everything, just as he took the very body he occupies. And I could do nothing to stop him.

"Then, after we married, he wanted a child, a beautiful child, one who would confirm his status as the new ruler of the land. I told him it wouldn't work, that human spirits like himself and Strangers such as I could not successfully mate. But he said I was merely trying to deceive him, that any child of ours was bound to be beautiful too. The wretched creature is vain beyond belief, and vanity is a nasty habit."

Yeah, sure. Her putting down vanity was like a rock star putting down publicity.

"In any case," she went on, "he ignored my pleading and got me with child. And he said he'd know I was trying to trick him if I brought forth a monster. He said he'd know it could be no child of his. Should that happen, he said, he'd put me to death, and then the Yelpers would enslave all my people.

"It happened, of course, as I had said it would. I gave birth to a deformed lump of flesh, shapeless, monstrous."

I couldn't see why it bothered her so much.

She'd invited a mixed bunch of more or less shapeless lumps of flesh over for the evening, hadn't she?

"The lives of all my people were in danger," she continued. "And so I did what I had to do. I sent one of my people, a willing volunteer, through the doorway, and I had your sister brought here. And I told the Hunter she was his child.

"He was willing to believe she was his, too—the human-minded fool didn't even bother to wonder why a newborn was already crawling. Oh yes, he was all too happy to leave me here with her and go off and do his hunting, have his vicious fun. I am in charge now, but I'm in his thrall nevertheless. And so Andrea is in *my* thrall. As long as the Hunter survives, I must keep Andrea here in order to protect my people. In order to protect myself."

"So," I said, "before I can get her back, I have to get rid of him? The Hunter?"

"Yes." She examined me again, sadly this time. "You. A mere child. It's not possible."

What looked like tears appeared in the corners of her regal eyes.

"Well, maybe it isn't," I said, thinking of those dogs in the park, their human heads, their sharp teeth, their claws, and that kid they'd tried to attack.

And trying not to think of Liam.

But then I looked over at Andrea sitting there on Mrs. F.'s lap, pulling on her nose and chortling away. "But at least I can try, can't I? I mean, there's no harm in trying."

"But there is, my lad," she said urgently. "There is great harm. What if you should fail? You will die, and die savagely. But more important, he'll know the attempt was made, and he'll quickly guess whose idea it was. He'll come after *me*."

And that was more important, was it? I pretended I hadn't noticed what she meant, and just said, "But he doesn't have to know whose idea it was, does he? I won't tell him, and why would you?"

She ignored my question. "Perhaps," she said again, musing. "Perhaps it's worth a try. Yes."

"Great," I said. "How will I do it?"

"First you'll have to find the Hunter. That part will be easy."

"It will?"

"Yes, once you demand your boon of me. Do it now. Do it loud, so everyone can hear. Shout, 'I demand my boon! I demand the White Cap!'"

So I did. I stood up, cleared my throat and said what she told me to say. Although what good some hat was going to do me was not clear at all.

Everyone in that huge room turned toward me as I shouted.

"No! No!" she said loudly, clutching her chest in this sort of melodramatic way. Well, she might be a queen, but she sure wasn't any actress. "Not that! Anything but that!" She winked at me, and then she whispered, "Insist. Make me do it."

"I . . . I insist," I said, rather lamely. "I must have the White Cap!" And then I added, "Please!" because my mom has told me to always be polite.

The queen gave me this sour look. She obviously didn't feel the same way about manners as my mom. Then she spoke in a very loud voice. "You subdue me with your forceful presence, brave sir. I must give in, against my will. The White Cap is yours!"

She turned to the guard stationed behind her and said, "Bring the White Cap!" And off he went to get it.

As everyone in the hall buzzed excitedly, the queen sat down. She gestured for that awful music to begin again, turned to me, and said, "Good. That's done."

"But what do I want this white hat for?"

"White Cap, human," she corrected me impatiently. "Don't you know anything? As every Stranger learns in nursery school, anyone who wears the White Cap may ask to go anywhere and will be taken there instantly. The Hunter and his band are off in your country wreaking devastation, as you well know. So first you leave my land, to some neutral place, of course. It's best not to leave a trail by going directly to him from here."

Of course not, I thought. That would put *you* in danger, wouldn't it? We can't have *that*, can we?

But it would also put Andrea in danger, and Mrs. F. I decided to go along with it.

"But once you are back in your own country," she continued, "you simply ask the White Cap to take you to him. And then . . ." She stopped and gave me this blank look. "And then it's up to you."

Now there was a long procession of servants coming toward us, the ones in front blaring on trumpets and then one carrying a red-velvet cushion. Sitting on the cushion was this little white beanie.

I kid you not. Just a beanie, like those little skull caps some Jewish kids wear.

The queen stood up, and with a dramatic gesture she picked up the beanie and placed it on my head. As she did, she said, "The White Cap is yours, fairly won. May it be fairly worn.

"And now," she said in a quieter voice to me alone, "you must leave, and leave quickly. The sooner you act, the less chance there is of discovery. Just tell it where you want to go—to your own country. To some *neutral* place."

So I went over and gave Andrea a kiss goodbye. And I shook hands with Mrs. F., who had been sitting there watching everything.

"All my thoughts will be with you, Johnny," she said in a worried voice.

I nodded and took a deep breath. There was no point delaying any longer. It was time to give that beanie a try.

"Take me, hat," I said. "Take me to my own country. Oh, yes, I almost forgot—to some neutral spot in my own country."

Sixteen

It was like being grabbed up in a tornado. I started spinning until I found myself lifting off the ground. Then the spinning got even faster, and I was going up and up, right through that shiny ceiling as if it wasn't even really there, and then up through the clouds.

And then I stopped spinning and landed.

And nearly fell over. I was being pushed by a strong wind, a cold strong wind. What now? Where was I? Snow was swirling around me, and it was hard to see, but as far as I could tell, I was in the middle of a field, a huge flat field. No buildings, no trees, nothing but snow and wind and darkness.

And cold. Suddenly I was very cold. Hardly surprising—it was the end of a cold winter night and I was somewhere in my own country, just like I'd asked. It obviously wasn't Riverview, but it had to be somewhere in Manitoba, where cold winter nights are pretty damn cold and the coldest places of all are the open prairies. I didn't even have my ski jacket on—it was still back there on the riverbank, where I'd used it as a towel. I had to get out of there, before I froze solid to the spot.

"No, you stupid hat," I shouted into the wind. "Take me to somewhere warmer."

But as I began to spin, I had second thoughts. I mean, I'd told the White Cap to bring me to my own country, and look what had happened—I was turning into a Nesbit-flavored popsicle. That stupid hat was just as tricky as everything else that had to do with Strangers, and I was going to have to be more cagey about what I said to it. I was going to have to be more specific.

My own house! Why not? It was safe and it was warm. With a happy vision of my cozy heated waterbed dancing in my head, I shouted, "Take me home. Take me to the warmest spot in my house."

The tornado came, and the wind and the snow disappeared, and then it felt really good—nice and warm. Hot, even.

Very hot.

I sat there enjoying the blissful heat as my eyes adjusted to the light. Finally I could see where I was. It sure didn't look like home. I was in some kind of tight enclosed space, and the light was coming from a tiny slit in front of me.

I bent forward and looked through the slit. I saw a washer and a dryer. Damn if it wasn't *our* washer and dryer, with *my* jeans hanging from the little clothesline my mom has there. I was home, all right. I was in the utility room in the basement.

To be more exact, in the furnace in the utility room in the basement.

Well, it *was* the warmest spot in the house— much warmer than the waterbed. Stupid hat.

And I had to get out of there fast, before the thermostat kicked in and the gas came through and the flames went on.

I tried to get out.

Guess what. There are no door handles on the insides of furnaces. Somebody should complain to the government. I mean, what kind of shoddy engineering is it that doesn't take into account the chance that a magical beanie might fly somebody inside of one every now and then, I'd like to know.

"Get me out of here, you stupid hat," I shouted. "Right now."

But I needed to tell it a destination.

Once more, I shouted the first thing that came into my head. "Take me to Sev!" I roared.

Yeah, Sev. Don't ask me why. Maybe it was because I was so hungry. And maybe my subconscious mind remembered that Sev was one of the few places in Riverview likely to be open at that time of night, because by now it was probably getting close to dawn.

As I stopped spinning this time, I came down for a landing right on top of a display in front of the cash register counter in Sev. Bags of sour-cream-and-onion-flavored tortilla chips went flying everywhere. Stupid hat.

But it was better than freezing or roasting, and I immediately decided it wasn't such a bad choice after all. For one thing, the people who work at Sev are so used to putting up with drunks and freaks and weirdos all night that they don't really notice anything or care about it even when they do notice it. Apparently the clerk hadn't even seen me landing in his tortilla chips.

Furthermore, I was hungry. And sure, the food they have there stinks. But I really was hungry.

So I was sitting in Sev in the middle of a scattered pile of tortilla-chip bags, actually making my saliva run by thinking about one of those godawful Big Bite hot dogs they sell there, when the clerk, who must have been at least half asleep, suddenly popped up from behind the counter and saw me. He got this nasty look on his ugly puss and said, "You again? I told you to beat it, kid, and I meant it."

"But . . ."

"I ain't selling you no cigarettes. You're too young and that's that. Out."

I got out. Fast. Because this time I'd figured it out right away. It had to be that Cowalker again, taking advantage of me going off to save the world and all to cruise the neighborhood ruining my reputation.

Trying to buy disgusting cigarettes, of all things.

I stood there shivering outside Sev on a cold winter morning, wishing I had my ski jacket with me and still thinking about how wonderful that Big Bite would have tasted. And I told myself I was going to have to close that damned door from Stranger country for sure. Just getting rid of the Cowalker was enough reason for doing it all by itself, without even needing to think about deranged beanies and green-toothed sex machines and near death by water and by fire in the space of a few short hours. Without even needing to think about Andrea.

As if it wasn't bad enough that the Cowalker had got me kicked out of Sev—where even druggies are welcome—I'd just remembered I wouldn't have been able to pay for that damned hot dog anyway. He'd already walked off with my allowance.

But as I got mad at the Cowalker, an idea started to form. I thought about the Cowalker, about how it walked around inside a body that looked like me. And that reminded me that the Hunter was walking around in a body that wasn't his either, that Yelpers like him stole the bodies of their victims. And I began to figure out how I might be able to trick the Hunter.

It might work, it just might. I mean, if Yelpers could move into different-looking bodies . . .

It was going to be dangerous. It was going to be scary. But it was all I could think of. I had to try it.

So I did. Right then, before I lost my courage

and talked myself out of it. I stood in front of Sev right there on Osborne Street in full view of the Saturday-morning traffic and shouted, "Okay, hat. Take me to where the Hunter is."

Just as the spinning began, I thought of something. "No, no," I said. "Wait, you stupid hat, wait." The spinning slowed down, and as I did slow pirouettes in the air, I said, "A slight change in the flight plan, Cap, old buddy. Take me to *near* where the Hunter is."

I was learning.

Seventeen

My good friend the hat decided that near the Hunter was right in the middle of the St. Vital bridge. On the roadway.

Luckily it was still pretty early in the morning and there wasn't all that much traffic. I got out of the path of a speeding Mazda and up onto the sidewalk as fast as I could, muttering impolite phrases at the hat under my breath, and I looked down over the river and into the park.

The hat was right. I *was* close to them. I could see the Hunter and his merry crew down in the park by the Monkey Paths. From this distance they looked just like a bunch of dogs sniffing around, but it was them, all right.

"Take me closer to where the Hunter is," I said, "and don't pull any fast ones."

I spun just a few times, very slowly. (Well, I'd told the hat not to pull any fast ones. So much for the warped sense of humor of your average magic headgear.) But at least it got me down into the park with only a few trees between me and those dogs.

I peeked out from behind a trunk. It was them for sure. They looked like dogs now, even their heads, but there was a mad look in their red eyes as they sniffed around.

I hunkered over and began to inch forward, trying to keep trees and shrubs between me and them, making sure my eyes were always on them.

The closer I got to them, the more human they got.

It was their faces that went first. One minute they were dogs sniffing the ground with their long black doggy snouts, and the next they were dogs with human faces sniffing the ground with their pink human schnozzes. Then they were just men in tattered-looking brown and black suits bent over and crawling around with their faces to the ground. Suddenly they all looked up at once, their heads pointed in my direction, their noses stuck up in the air and sniffing away. They looked totally ridiculous.

And totally scary.

But it was obvious they knew I was there, and I was eventually going to have to show myself anyway if I wanted my plan to work. I stood up.

As I did and they caught sight of me, they began to waver in and out of focus in a weird way. They looked like dogs, then humans, then dogs again. They seemed to be uncertain about how they wanted me to see them.

Then, I guess, the Hunter finally decided I'd already seen them as humans, so they couldn't fool me into believing they were dogs. He made a quick gesture with his paw, or hand, and they all stopped wavering and became humans.

Ugly, dangerous-looking humans. They would have felt right at home standing around in front of Sev. They formed a tight group behind the Hunter as he moved toward me.

He was the toughest-looking one of the lot, the Hunter was—one freaky-looking dude. I wondered where he'd got that body in the first place. The guy who'd originally had it—been born into it—must have really been something.

From a distance he just looked like this big hairy guy with lots of muscles packed into a tacky brown suit. But as he got closer to me, I began to pick out some interesting details.

His hair was knotted and braided and filled with jewels that sparkled in the sunlight, like some rapper freak in a music video. His cheeks above his great huge beard were streaked yellow, green, blue, and red, and the streaks went down into the beard. War paint, I guess, or else he was a very messy eater.

But his eyes were the weirdest. They gleamed and glistened and sparkled like twinkling Christmas tree lights, and I finally figured out why. He had six or seven pupils in each eye.

As he came forward, I managed to tear my gaze away from his eyes long enough to notice that he was holding the horn in one of his hands—a hand that had what looked like too many fingers on it. I couldn't help myself, in spite of my fear. I counted them. There were seven—seven on each hand.

I went into my act.

"Don't hurt me, mister," I said, putting on this whining, little-kid voice. "Don't hurt me! I was just watching. I didn't do nothing wrong!" The bad grammar was a nice touch, I thought, and on this cold morning, I didn't even have to pretend to quiver and shiver and quake.

He gave me this long, cool look, as if he couldn't believe any kid was as dumb as I was pretending to be— so dumb that I hadn't even noticed how truly bizarre he looked. He finally seemed to decide that I *was* just some dumb ungrammatical kid who didn't know who he was or how dangerous he was.

"Nobody's going to hurt you, sonny," he said in this growly voice.

Good. He'd bought it. He must have been almost as dumb as I was pretending to be.

"Golly, mister," I said, making my eyes go big and round. "What a neat horn! Boy, oh, boy, I wish *I* had a horn like that!"

His eyes lit up, all twelve or fourteen pupils sparkling. "You do, do you?" he asked, giving me this sneaky-looking smile. The other Yelpers milling in a tight group behind him started to snicker a little, until the Hunter silenced them with a quick gesture.

It was working. They were beginning to think that maybe they had another tasty meal on their hands.

"I bet that horn makes a good loud noise when you blow into it," I said. "I like loud noises!"

"It does," he said, smiling again. "A very loud noise. Would you like to try it?"

"Golly!" I said. "Could I, mister? Could I really try it?"

"Sure you can, my good lad," he said, and he held the horn out to me in his many-fingered hand.

"Wow." I took the horn and raised it to my lips. I could hear pants of anticipation, and as I looked from the corner of my eye at the Yelpers milling behind the Hunter, I could see the transformation begin once more. Their eyes were going red again, and hair was growing on their faces. And the sun began to glint off the fangs that were now coming out of their mouths.

"Foolish is he who blows the horn of the Hunter." I could hear Liam's words echoing over and over inside my head, but I did it anyway. I blew the Hunter's horn, knowing that the Yelpers would be on me as soon as my breath entered it and made a sound. But I told myself I had a trick up my sleeve. I told myself I knew what I was doing, and I willed myself to do it. I blew, desperately hoping that the trick would work. Because if it didn't work, I really was going to be dead meat.

Dead and already on the menu. Today's special.

I blew—one long, loud, piercing note. And then, damn it, everything went wrong.

It all happened far faster than I'd expected. The Yelpers were dogs already, and they were beginning to leap toward me, the Hunter in front of the rest. He was a dog himself now, a huge dog with seven pupils in each eye, and he had raised up his front paws, paws with too many long sharp claws on them.

A dog, leaping at me in a fury. Before I could move or think, he was almost at my throat.

It was too late, too late to do anything. So much for my trick. I was doomed.

But then, just as I could almost feel the pressure of those sharp teeth against my skin, I heard a noise. A high-pitched scream. And the Hunter suddenly lurched out of his path and whizzed by me.

It wasn't too late yet after all!

As I braced myself and waited for the Hunter to turn back to me again, I realized what had happened. One of the other Yelpers had suddenly shrieked and knocked the Hunter aside, bodychecked the Hunter, and then gone flying off up into the sky. It had only been for the briefest of moments, but it had been long enough to keep me alive to work my plan. Why had that Yelper turned on his boss like that?

Well, there was no time to worry about it. The Hunter was already hurtling toward me again with an enraged growl emerging from between his curled lips. As quickly as I could, I pulled the horn from my mouth and shouted, "Take me inside the Hunter, little buddy." I hoped with all my will that the hat would understand what I meant and not play any dumb tricks.

It didn't. For once, it did exactly what I wanted. It probably thought it finally had me just where it wanted me, in deep, deep trouble.

And maybe I was in deep trouble. Suddenly I was no longer looking at a huge angry dog lunging toward me, its claws raised and its fangs exposed. Instead I was looking at this terrified-looking kid, this kid holding a gleaming horn and wearing a silly-looking white beanie.

I was looking at myself.

I was looking at myself again and again, for I seemed to be seeing many different images at once with my many-pupiled eyes.

It had worked. I was inside the Hunter, inside his head.

Best of all, the Hunter wasn't with me. My trick had worked as I'd hoped it would. It was a pretty puny brain, after all, and I guess there was just room for one of us in there. At any rate, as the hat had forced me in, it had squeezed him out. I was him now, just the way that Cowalker was me. I was inside the Hunter's body and in his mind, seeing through his eyes and feeling with his many fingers.

And the Hunter? Well, the Hunter was a Yelper, after all. And like Liam had told me, he couldn't bear to be a spirit without a body, doomed to float disembodied through the worlds. He needed a body. And there was only one available.

And so he took it, as I'd hoped he would—as I'd dreaded he would. As my fangs approached what had just a few seconds earlier been my own neck, I could see he was in there, could see the look of hatred he was sending out through my eyes. My former eyes.

That look—it totally changed the face, changed it so it didn't look like me anymore. It was a look of hatred—pure, evil hatred. But somehow it was gleeful, too, happy about hating.

I was enraged.

Enraged by that look.

Enraged at what the Hunter had almost done to that innocent little kid, here on this very spot just a few days ago.

Enraged about what he *had* done to the queen, and at what had happened to Andrea and Mrs. F. as a result of it.

And I guess that body of his, that mad-dog body I was now inside, was having something to say about it, too—exciting me, urging me on. I totally forgot it was my own body I was leaping on, my own neck I was going for.

I attacked.

I threw myself upon him, fangs and claws exposed. And . . .

And for some time after that there's a blank. I have no memory of it.

And I don't want to have any memory of it. Not ever.

When I came back to myself again, I was standing there with the rest of the Yelpers, panting over what had once been my own body. I stood there panting, satiated, this delicious and yet repulsive taste in my mouth.

As I stood there, I could feel myself becoming human again. My fangs were getting shorter, my fur sparser.

As soon as my paw turned into a hand, I reached out almost without thinking and grabbed the white beanie off the ground where it had fallen. It was in pretty good shape, considering. Only a few splashes of blood on it.

I was myself again.

But not quite myself.

I was in the Hunter's body now. I had extra eyes and extra fingers and a whole lot of extra hair.

And he, if he was still alive, he was in what was left of my body. As I looked down at it, I realized I was a whole lot better off with a few extra fingers. Better too many than too few.

I had that Yelper to thank for it, the one who'd shoved the Hunter aside at the last minute. Why had he done it?

Now that I had time to think about it, I remembered that Yelper's scream again. A shriek. A high-pitched squeal. It reminded me of something. Of someone.

It reminded me of Liam.

Could it have been? Could it really have been Liam? Had he somehow turned into a Yelper?

It was possible. Even though I'd tried not to admit it, I'd known all along that the other shriek, the one I'd heard before out by the sewer, had to be Liam. Couldn't have been anything else.

And Yelpers stole the bodies of their prey. It seemed logical that one of them might have tried to take over Liam's body.

But a Yelper spirit in Liam's body wouldn't care about me, would it? It didn't make sense.

Unless Liam was still somehow in that body. He was a Stranger himself, after all—not a human. Maybe his Stranger spirit had taken over from the Yelper instead of the other way around. Or maybe his body just somehow remembered me, tried to save me.

He *had* saved me. Maybe he wasn't a wimp. Maybe he had become a human after all, just as he'd wanted.

And somewhere, it seemed, he was still alive. Alive and alone, and locked up in that dog's existence.

Poor Liam.

As I'd been thinking about Liam, the Yelpers were gradually coming back to their human forms again. They stood there licking the blood off their chins with now-human tongues, and they looked at me expectantly. I was the Hunter, or so they imagined. I was their leader. They expected me to lead them.

And we obviously couldn't stand there milling around the remains of our feast, waiting for the cops to show up. I decided to give the order to fly while I thought about what to do next.

"Okay, you guys," I said, "we're out of here."

Instead of flying, they all gave me these looks, and began to growl and sidle off. Somehow they guessed immediately that I wasn't the Hunter.

"All right," I said, accepting the inevitable, "you got it. Right the first time. I'm not the Hunter. That was him you just did in. I made the switch just before the attack. Tough luck, dudes."

By now they were really growling, growling like dogs again and beginning to circle around me, but still confused, because I looked like the Hunter.

"If you're looking for the Hunter, he's in there. Or at least," I added, looking down again at that repulsive mess and then quickly turning away from it, "that *was* the Hunter."

They turned from me and gathered around the remains of their feast and sniffed. And then, I guess, they must have smelled the Hunter in there, and they knew it was true. They all began to howl, howl in this agonized way as they realized what they'd done. They'd attacked their own master.

I knew I'd better get out of there quick. They were mourning now, lost in their grief. But soon they'd begin to wonder what had happened. They probably wouldn't be able to figure it out, but they'd know it was my fault, and they'd be after me. They had no leader, but they were still Sky Yelpers.

I jammed the White Cap, which I'd been holding in my hand, down over my greasy hair. It caught on some of those jewels, but I managed to get it on enough to stay.

Then, as quietly and sneakily as I could, I inched my way into that mob howling around the remains and, keeping my eyes turned away so I wouldn't have to look at the mess and get sick again, I grabbed the horn.

I figured I needed proof for the queen that the Hunter was gone.

I grabbed the horn and at the same time shouted, "Okay, hat, take me to—" And stopped. Take me to where?

Thinking about it now, I suppose I could have gone back to the queen right then and there. That would have been the smart thing to do. I mean, with the Hunter gone, I didn't think I had to worry anymore about endangering her precious majesty by leaving a trail. But for some reason I wasn't thinking very clearly—a good thing, as it turned out.

And I had to get out of there fast. The Yelpers had heard my shout and were looking up at me.

"Take me to my house!" I said, and then, realizing the beanie might be confused about just who I was in my current condition, I added, "Johnny Nesbit's house. On Wavell Avenue in Riverview. In the kitchen, please. On the floor. In front of the fridge." Surely that was specific enough.

Well, Mom and Dad were definitely not going to appreciate me coming home in this state, with four extra fingers and twelve extra pupils and a lot more hair on my face and elsewhere than I'd ever managed to produce yet. They were definitely going to think I was getting in with a bad crowd.

But you know what people say: any port in a storm.

Eighteen

As I landed in the kitchen—in front of the fridge, on the floor, just like I'd said—Mom was standing over by the stove stirring stuff in a pot, talking over her shoulder to somebody sitting at the table. The person at the table was hunched over a bowl, spooning and slurping, paying no attention to the thing that looked like Andrea in the baby seat on the table beside him.

The person at the table was me.

No, I remembered with a sick feeling in my gut. I didn't look like that anymore. I looked a lot more *interesting* than that.

It was that Cowalker. It was wearing my bathrobe and those dumb-looking beaded moccasins my Auntie Kay and Uncle Bob gave me last Christmas.

Trust it to pick *those* creepy things out of my closet.

But other than the moccasins and the fact that it was eating oatmeal again, the Cowalker could have been me. The old me.

Well, at least one of us was looking like the old me. I sure wasn't—as I realized as soon as I came to a halt in front of the fridge. Because at that moment Mom glanced over, saw me, gave a huge shriek, and fainted dead away.

Well, it's not all that often that a biker type with a passion for accessorizing suddenly appears in your kitchen.

The Cowalker was a little less excited. It gave me a brief bored look and then went right back to wolfing down the oatmeal.

It was then that I got the idea. I didn't want to spend my whole life looking like a reject from WWF wrestling. I wanted my own body back. It wasn't much, I guess, but I was used to it.

And if that trick had worked with the Hunter, why not with this guy?

I shouted, "Take me inside the Cowalker," and immediately I was there, looking out from what seemed to be my old familiar one-pupiled eyes at the body of the Hunter, which now had no spirit in it and so was slowly slumping down to the floor in front of the fridge.

"Bug off, buddy," I heard a voice say. It was coming from all around me. "This is mine," it said. "I was here first."

Maybe this wasn't going to be so easy after

all. I guess the Hunter had been so surprised when I came into his head that he'd been pushed out right away, but this guy hadn't reacted that quickly. He was still there. And wanting to stay there, too.

"But you stole it from me," I said. "It was my image in the first place."

"Big deal," he said. "You left it there in the mirror without any protection. Finders, keepers."

I could see I was going to have to be a little more cagey. Either that or spend the rest of my days arguing with this obnoxious creep inside my own head.

"Look," I said, "there's no reason for a fight. We've got two perfectly good bodies here. I'll make you a trade. If you give me this body, I'll let you have that one over there." I forced our head to turn in the direction of the Hunter's body in front of the fridge.

"Well," he said thoughtfully, "it's not bad-looking, I'll grant you that. A lot better than this wimpy thing."

I willed myself to keep my cool.

"And don't forget the life-style," I told him. "You choose that fine-looking, definitely non-wimpy body over there, and no more taking the garbage out. No more memorizing irregular French verbs. No more cleaning your room. Instead, you get to be boss of a whole gang. You just sit back and relax, and the gang waits on you hand and foot and provides you with all the food you could ever want."

I neglected to mention that the food wasn't oatmeal.

"Hmmm," it said, making our eyes give the Hunter's body a good going-over. "Nice hair. Is it in good shape?"

"Gets good mileage both on the ground and in the air," I assured him. "And it has all the options, too. Extra pupils in the eyes, extra fingers. Good teeth. And if you should ever get tired of all that stuff, you can turn into a dog whenever you want."

"Hmmm." He made us walk over to the Hunter's body, gave it a kick in the stomach, and said, "Solid. There's still a few good years left in that."

Then he looked again and thought some more.

Finally he said, "Okay, you're on. I'll take it. You can have this useless thing if you really want it. Good riddance to bad rubbish, I say. When you're in *this* dumb thing, they won't even let you have any smokes. And I sure don't envy you the mother, even if she does make good oatmeal."

The next thing I knew, I was alone inside my head, getting mad at the Cowalker. That was my mom he was talking about. Just who did he think he was anyway?

But I didn't have time to think about it. The Hunter's body was reviving again.

Quickly, before the Cowalker was able to do anything about it, I snatched the white hat off his head and jammed it on what was now my own. My own head. I couldn't believe how good it felt.

"Hey, no fair," the Cowalker said in the Hunter's deep voice. "I thought the Cap came with it."

"I never said it did. Or this either," I added, grabbing the horn out of his hand.

And before he could get mad about it and remember he had all those claws and teeth, I said, "If you want that gang I told you about, you'll have to hurry."

He nodded, and I took him out the back door and gave him instructions for getting down to the Monkey Paths. Then I said good-bye (and good riddance) and went into the living room to watch through the big window as he strolled nonchalantly down Wavell, his jewel-covered hair waving around him in the bright morning sunlight. He would be quite a surprise for anyone who happened to glance outside. Or maybe not. They'd probably just think he was yet another religious nut looking for converts and decide not to answer the doorbell if it rang.

None of this had taken very long, and when I got back to the kitchen Mom was still lying on the floor unconscious. I decided that the best thing to do was just leave her there. She'd wake up soon anyway, and when she did, she'd probably think she just imagined the whole thing.

At least I hoped so. I really didn't have time to think about it. I didn't even have time to think about how lucky I was to get my own body back. I had other things to do.

I remembered I had other things to do when I glanced over at the thing that was supposed to be Andrea, still sitting there by the table in the baby seat. I looked, but I didn't see Andrea.

I saw a grotesquely wrinkled little creature, a bald little hairy man with a huge red nose with warts on it.

For some reason, whatever it was that had made the Changeling look like Andrea before wasn't working anymore. I wondered why, but not for long. The most urgent thing was just to get that repulsive thing out of my house and out of my life once and for all.

So I stuffed the horn inside the front of my bathrobe and then once more—one last time, I hoped—I spoke to the white beanie on my head.

"Take me back to the queen's castle, hat!" I shouted.

And it did.

Nineteen

The castle didn't look the same. Oh, it was the same place all right—same huge room, same fireplace, same murky darkness with people dancing in it. But it was different, totally different.

The last time I'd been there, it had been clean, new, sparkling. Now it was old and decrepit, the tapestries on the walls threadbare, the floor scuffed and scratched. The ceiling still glowed above me, but somehow, you know, it didn't look like diamonds anymore. More like that Home Shopping Channel cubic zirconia stuff.

And the dancers? Well, the weird ones, the wisps of flame and the giants with two heads and all—they still looked the same. But before, mixed in with the weird ones there had been all these handsome guys and great-looking babes in expensive-looking clothes. They were still there now, and they still acted like they had before, talking and laughing and dancing. But now they were wrinkled and bent over and covered with strange rashes and skin diseases, and their fancy clothes were torn and patched.

Up there on that platform, the queen sat at her banquet. The table in front of her was still covered with plates, but now the plates were filled with green beans. Nothing but green beans, where I'd seen all that tasty-looking food before.

The queen herself still looked queenly. She still had that bossy look on her face. And I could still recognize the face, sort of. It was the same face, but the same face as it might look after a few hundred years or so had passed. She looked old. Very old.

Even Mrs. F., who sat there by the queen, looked kind of worn and tired. And there was this sickly tinge of green to Mrs. F.'s skin.

Why had everything changed so much?

As I glanced around, I saw with relief that one thing hadn't changed. It was Andrea. The real Andrea—not a wrinkle or a wart in sight. She was perched on Mrs. F.'s lap, cooing and smiling and looking like a healthy, happy baby.

My excitement about getting her back took over from my confusion about all the changes, and I stepped up to the queen.

"So you're back, are you, my lad?" she said. "And so soon, too. Given up already?"

"No, your majesty," I said sharply. "I'm sorry to disappoint you, but I'm not defeated. I won, in fact."

The look on her face changed totally.

"And," I added, bowing low before her, "I present you with"—and I pulled it out from inside my bathrobe—"the horn of the Hunter."

"The horn!" She eyed it greedily, then stepped forward and took it. As she did so, she lifted her head and gazed into my eyes.

"He . . . he's gone, then?"

"Yes, your majesty. He's gone."

"The Hunter, gone. I . . . I hardly dare to believe it." She grabbed my arm and pulled me toward her. "Tell me about it. Tell me all about it."

After I had finished, the queen was silent for a moment, mulling it over.

"Yes," she finally said, "I believe he *is* gone. Gone, or as good as gone. Few spirits could survive an attack of the Yelpers, and even if the Hunter's spirit has survived, it's homeless now. He has no body to inhabit and, without his cohorts, no power to find a way back into one. He can do nothing but wander the worlds, wander forever alone, unable to communicate with other beings. Good.

"And the Yelpers," she continued thoughtfully. "Their power, too, is less. Not only will they mourn their leader's death and their own part in it, but that Cowalker doesn't sound like the sort who'll incite them to violence."

Nope, I thought. It's more likely he'll have them searching the worlds for oatmeal.

"Yes, my lad," she continued. "You've done well. I am free. You have earned your boon."

"You know what I want, your majesty," I said quickly, looking over at Andrea.

"Yes, I know. You've earned it. Go now and take her."

As I reached down to take Andrea, Mrs. F. whispered in my ear, "Be careful, Johnny. Don't forget to be careful. And whatever happens, hold on tight."

What did she mean? I had every intention of holding on tight. It was my sister, after all.

I took Andrea from Mrs. F. and hugged her, and felt happy as Andrea looked up at me and cooed—so happy I held her even tighter.

Which was a good thing, because Andrea suddenly began to vibrate, faster and faster. In my surprise, I almost loosened my grip. But then I remembered Mrs. F.'s whisper, and I tightened it again.

And then Andrea changed.

I was holding on to a huge gooey pancreas or something—a huge pancreas with giant teeth about to chomp down on me. It was scary. But not all that scary, and by now I was really ready for anything. I held on.

The pancreas vibrated and became softer, smoother. I was holding a gorgeous girl, a naked gorgeous girl with blue eyes and flowing black hair and pointy green teeth. I couldn't help wanting to hold her. I hated wanting to hold her and I wanted to let her go. But I held on tight.

The girl lost her skin. I was holding on to her veins and arteries and bones and all. Blood dripped from my fingers. I nearly barfed, but I didn't let go.

The skinless girl vibrated and became a dog. A dog with a human head and dog fangs, the fangs snapping at me. I recognized that dog even though I'd never seen it before, recognized it by the horrible sound of its panting in my ear. It was the hag— the hag that had ridden me those mornings while I was lying under the sheets. I closed my eyes and gritted my teeth, and held on tight.

The dog vibrated and became Jason. Jason Garrett, that pushy creep from my school. I was standing there in front of everybody in the castle hugging Jase, holding him as tight as I could. As I held him, he bent over and planted this loud kiss right on my lips.

I almost did let go that time. Then I told myself it was really just magic, really just Andrea. It had to be Andrea, didn't it? My stomach churned, but I held on tight.

Jase vibrated and turned into—well, I don't know how to describe it, exactly. Jason turned into a huge pile of turds. A smelly disgusting heap of turds, coating me, dripping everywhere. It wasn't all that much of a change, really. I screwed up my nose, and I concentrated with all my might on nothing but holding on.

And the turds turned into—

Andrea.

Twenty

I was holding Andrea again. Andrea looking a little confused, but still Andrea.

I was holding my baby sister. Holding her tight. I was happy.

Andrea herself wasn't looking all that happy, though. She looked at me accusingly, as if she couldn't understand why big people were always doing dumb things to her. Then she sighed and nestled down.

"What happened?" I said to the queen. "It was a spell, wasn't it? You put a spell on her!"

"Of course I did," said the queen calmly. "My safety depended on her, after all. I had to protect her from thieves in order to protect myself."

I was furious. "Then why didn't you tell me about it before you gave her to me?"

She gave me a perplexed look, as if I'd said something really odd. "Why would I? It was your business, my lad, not mine. And anyway," she added, "what's the problem? You won her in spite of my little spell, didn't you? Your will was strong enough to break it."

My will had been strong enough to break the spell. My will had won Andrea back. Just wait till Mom heard.

"And now," said the queen, "I am getting more than a little bored with all this. Your business here is finished. You must take the child and go. Now."

It sounded good to me. Nothing would make me happier than to get Andrea out of there and home, where—

Where that thing was still sitting in the baby seat.

The ointment. I'd forgotten about the fairy ointment I'd come for in the first place. Without it, taking Andrea back home wasn't going to do any good. My folks would just think she was a different baby, a baby who looked like ours but really wasn't. No, they'd only accept her as herself when the Changeling was gone. And the Changeling wouldn't leave as long as my parents kept on believing it was actually Andrea. I needed that ointment so they could see the truth.

And the queen was just about to let me head off home without it. She was a Stranger, all right. You couldn't trust her for an instant.

But she wasn't getting away with it this time.

"Before I go," I told her, "I'll be needing some ointment. Some fairy ointment."

She looked a little startled. "Ointment? How did you know about fairy ointment, human?"

Well, I couldn't see any harm in telling her. "Liam told me. Liam Green, this friend of mine back home."

"And how did this . . . this Liam person know about it?"

I tried to remember what Liam had told me. "From his foster father, I think. Yeah, Mr. Rhymer told him."

The queen started, and grabbed my arm. "Mr. Rhymer? *Thomas* Rhymer?"

"Uh, yes. I think so."

"Thomas Rhymer! After all these years! Remarkable!" said the queen.

"Yeah," I said, not understanding why she was getting so excited. "Anyway, I suppose I have to win the ointment somehow, too, right?"

"Good gracious, no," she said. "Do you think I'm ungrateful? Human beings are so peculiar. No, human, the ointment is yours if you want it."

She reached into a pocket in her skirt, took out a little bottle, and handed it to me.

"And now," she said, "you must say farewell to your friend."

My friend? She meant Mrs. F.

"Can't . . . can't she come, too?"

"Good gracious, no," the queen said off-handedly. "*She* is ours for eternity. She has eaten our food."

So that was it. So that was what Mrs. F. had meant before when she told me not to eat. She'd saved my life.

And Andrea's life, too. I remembered her telling me that Andrea had never had anything but breast milk, the first time I saw her inside the hill. She hadn't let Andrea eat any of their food either.

I wanted Mrs. F. to come back with me, too. There had to be some way.

But before I could ask the queen, I heard a voice behind me. "She's right, John." It was Mrs. F., who had come up to where I was standing with Andrea in my arms. "There's nothing you can do, nothing. I have to stay. But you mustn't feel bad about it. I'm getting used to it, I really am. I'm beginning to feel like one of them. I'll be okay here."

It was unfair. I couldn't just desert her, could I?

But I had to. I had no choice. There are some things you just have to accept, no matter how strong your will is.

And to tell the truth, I was even a little relieved. I mean, I would have had some pretty fancy explaining to do if I'd suddenly shown up back home with Mrs. F. in tow. Mrs. F., returned from the grave and looking kind of green.

Not that I wouldn't have gone through the trouble if saving her was possible. It just wasn't possible. I had to accept it.

So I did. I just said, "Thanks, Mrs. F. Thanks for your help." Andrea reached out and babbled at her, and Mrs. F. leaned forward and kissed Andrea on the cheek, and then grabbed her hand and held it tight for a while. Then she dropped the hand and quickly turned her head and moved away.

And I never saw her again.

"Now, human," said the queen. "One last thing. You must deliver a message for me."

A message, after all those tricks she'd played on me? Well, you couldn't say she didn't have nerve.

"This is my message," she said, and she handed me the horn I'd given her—the horn I'd gone through so much trouble to get. "You need do nothing more than to take the horn to Thomas—to Mr. Rhymer. He will understand."

Well, I didn't get it. But it sounded easy enough. "Okay," I said. I took the horn back and stuck it inside my bathrobe again.

"And now," she said, "you must return the White Cap."

"Return it?" I'd been expecting to use it. "Then how will we get home?"

"I will arrange it," she said. "The Cap, please."

I gave her the beanie. I can't say I was all that sad to see the underhanded little rascal go.

Then she lifted her hands into the air and shouted some strange words I didn't understand. A blinding light began to appear all around us, low down, just at the point where the floor of the castle met the walls.

The light grew, and it began to be reflected in that shiny ceiling high above us. Soon the ceiling was dazzling, and I found it hard to see anything at all.

As I stood there blinking, my eyes began to adjust. Past where the walls had been, I could make out trees and sunshine, and what looked like snow.

It *was* snow. It *was* trees. And out past them, cars going by. Traffic.

The walls of the castle had lifted, raised up on columns, and outside was . . . Winnipeg. Portage Avenue, it looked like, in the heart of downtown.

"Farewell, human," said the queen, and she gestured for me to leave. So I did.

As I stepped out into the snow, I turned around and looked back at the castle. It was sitting up there in midair suspended on pillars, with all that light pouring out of it.

Then the pillars descended down into the ground, and the castle came down out of the sky. It looked just the way it had the first time I saw it.

Which was weird. I was expecting it to disappear altogether, but it didn't. It just sat there looking out of place—cars and buses rushing by on Portage Avenue in front of it, while it looked for all the world as if some damsel in distress might suddenly lean out a window in one of the towers and yell for help.

As I shivered there in my bathrobe, holding Andrea and feeling very confused, I took a few steps backward in the snow to get a clearer view of the castle, and bumped into something. It was a big sign. A large map of a building floor plan inside a glass case.

The University of Winnipeg, it said above the map.

The University of Winnipeg. Of course. I remembered thinking that the Stranger castle had looked familiar the first time I saw it, and now I suddenly realized why. It looked just like the big old building at the front of the University of Winnipeg, downtown on Portage Avenue.

And apparently we *were* downtown on Portage Avenue. Andrea and I had walked out of the castle in Stranger country and ended up on the front lawn of the University of Winnipeg.

Twenty-one

I looked at the building again, more confused than before. It was the same building, all right, except now the moat was gone, and the bridge. Oh, and there were sidewalks leading up to it, and there were other buildings all around, and there was all that traffic out there. It was the same, and it was totally different. If a damsel in distress did lean out of a window now, it would probably be because she wanted help with her trigonometry.

And it was cold out, bitter cold, and the light clothes Andrea was wearing weren't even as thick as my bathrobe. If we didn't get inside quick, we were both going to freeze. The U of W was as good a place as any.

Maybe better, I realized, as I headed up the sidewalk to that big arched door. It was a public place, and it'd be open even on a Saturday morning. And I suddenly remembered that Rhymer guy worked there—the old man Liam lived with, the guy I was supposed to take the horn to. He was a folklore professor at the University of Winnipeg. And hey, maybe that was why the queen made us come here, because Rhymer was inside somewhere, grading tests or whatever it is professors do when they're not boring people to death with their lectures.

I stepped inside, almost afraid it'd turn back into the Stranger castle again. But there wasn't a dancing flame in sight. It was just a normal building now. Depressingly normal. The walls of the entryway I found myself standing in were covered in this stupid rec-room paneling that's supposed to look old-fashioned but doesn't, and as for the ceiling, well, there was no cubic zirconia in sight.

After warming up a little, Andrea and I wandered up and down stairways and through corridor after corridor, looking for some sign of Rhymer. The rec-room paneling soon disappeared and gave way to endless long halls lined with beige bricks and closed doors, like some giant insurance agency. I smiled bravely at the few people I passed, desperately pretending that it was quite normal for a kid to be wandering around in the university on a Saturday morning with a baby and a bathrobe and the world's ugliest moccasins on.

Finally, in a hallway where the doors were even closer together than usual, I came upon one that said Dr. Thomas Rhymer on it. I knocked.

After a few moments, the door opened, and the oldest man I have ever seen popped his head out. A few wisps of white hair on an almost-bald head, a white face filled with wrinkles. He looked even older than the Stranger queen.

"Mr. Rhymer?" The old man nodded. "My name is Johnny Nesbit," I said, "and I've brought you a message." I reached into my bathrobe and pulled out the horn. "The queen said you'd understand."

He looked at that horn, his eyes gleaming.

"Yes," he whispered. "Oh, yes. I understand. A Stranger object! Oh, thank you, my lad, thank you. Come in, come in." Tears were glistening in his eyes as his bony old fingers clutched at my arm and dragged me inside.

It was a tiny office, just big enough for a desk and some chairs, with a terrific view of the bus depot parking structure across the street. It was lined with shelves and most of them were covered with old books and papers.

But what immediately drew my eyes was on the shelves just behind the desk. It was all these things. Old crowns filled with jewels. Antique swords. Fancy belts and brooches and hats. And an entire set of old-fashioned clothes, leggings and a top and all. A huge treasure—it must be worth a fortune.

But as I looked more closely, I could see that it was all paper. They were amazing replicas, detailed down to the smallest of folds. But they were still just paper.

"Johnny Nesbit," the old man said, staring at me from behind the desk. "Young Liam told me about you. And you have the horn—and, I see, the baby." He smiled at Andrea, showing all these yellow teeth. "So your quest has been successful. I am glad. Sit." He gestured toward a chair. "Sit, and tell me all about it."

As I sat down and adjusted Andrea on my knee, I suddenly realized how grateful I was that Mr. Rhymer was there. I needed to tell somebody about it, just to hear the words coming out of my mouth and confirm for myself that it had all really happened. And there was nobody else in the whole known universe who was going to believe me, except for him.

He listened carefully as I told him about it all, nodding every once in a while. For some reason he was really pleased when I told him about how the Hunter had treated the queen, and then even more pleased when I told him what I'd done to the Hunter.

I saved Liam for last. I was afraid he'd get upset when he heard about that, really upset. After all, Liam was sort of like a son to him. And Mr. Rhymer was so old, so frail. Who knew what finding out about Liam might do to him?

It did nothing.

"Yes," he said calmly. "I think you're right. Liam is a Yelper now. Poor fellow never could accept himself for what he was, and look where it got him." He smiled again, showing those yellow teeth.

"But . . ." I was confused. Didn't he care about Liam at all? "Won't you, well, miss him?"

"Miss him?" He seemed really surprised by my question. But then he nodded. "Oh, yes, yes, of course. I suppose so.

"But you, John Nesbit," he went on in a much more hearty voice, *"you* have done well, very well indeed. The Hunter is defeated, damn his black soul. The baby is back, and the door will soon be closed. And soon, soon, I shall . . ." He paused, smiling happily at the horn he held in his hand. "Very well, indeed," he said again.

He looked up at us again. "But now, my boy, time's a-wasting. You must take that child home to your mother and father." Then he seemed to really notice the way we looked for the first time. "Good heavens," he said with a frown, "you can't go out in that bitter cold in those flimsy garments and those ridiculous moccasins. I'll call you a taxi."

I tried to stop him, but he insisted on it. He even gave me a twenty to cover the fare. "After all," he said as he lovingly fondled the horn, "I won't be needing it myself now." And he giggled in this strange, gleeful way.

The guy on the phone said it would take a while for the cab to arrive, which gave me a chance to ask Mr. Rhymer about something that was really bothering me—something I was almost afraid to ask.

"No," he answered. "You have no cause to worry. Yes, to be sure, that's a Stranger body you have. That's probably why you can see through the Stranger deceptions. You have Stranger eyes. But even though it's a Stranger body, it started out as your image in the mirror. That's why you're left-handed now, instead of right-handed."

I was, too, I realized. I was holding that twenty in my left hand.

"And that body's inhabited by a human now," he

went on. "The longer you live in it, the more human it will become."

I'd never felt so relieved in my life. I was myself again, more or less.

"So really," Rhymer said with this strange embarrassed look on his face, "there's no real damage, is there? I . . . I do hope you'll forgive me."

"Forgive *you*?" What did he have to do with it?

"Yes. Me." He suddenly blushed bright red. "Because . . . because it was all my fault, you see. The door was left open because of me."

Because of him? Because of some tired old professor?

"I don't get it," I said.

"To understand," he said, "you must know my story." And so, as we sat there waiting for the cabbie to knock on the door, he told me about himself.

It was an amazing story. Hearing it was like taking off your sunglasses outside on a sunny winter day. Suddenly everything seemed different.

He had been born long ago, he said—almost eight hundred years ago.

Eight hundred years, I swear, that's what he told me. Yeah, sure, and Pepsi really does taste different from Coke.

But when you looked at him, you know, at his wrinkles and pasty skin and all, it wasn't so hard to believe.

Anyway, one day when he was a young man, the queen of the Strangers saw him strolling in the countryside—the same queen I'd just said good-bye to. She saw him and she wanted him and, as usual, she took what she wanted. She spirited him off to her country, and he lived there with her for seven years. Lived happily, he said, for he loved her.

As he told me that, I suddenly heard the queen's voice inside my head. "My consort," it said. So Mr. Rhymer was the consort—the consort who'd left.

He'd left because this thing called the Teind fell due. It was a sort of tax that the fairies owed to a dark power in return for their own safety. The Strangers feared that dark power the way human beings used to fear Strangers, and they willingly paid up. The trouble was, the Teind was paid in the form of a human spirit, and the queen was afraid the Stranger court would insist on sending Mr. Rhymer, him being already in their country and so handily available and all. So she made him go home, planning to bring him back as soon as the Teind had been paid in some other way, in a few weeks or so. He was to wait for her to send him a Stranger object, something he would know had come from Stranger country, as a signal for his return. And that's when the door was left open.

"So you see," Mr. Rhymer said, "it *was* my fault."

The queen sent Mr. Rhymer home to England with farewell gifts—a rich treasure. But the treasure turned out to be worthless. "All these things you see here are part of it," he said, pointing at the paper things on the shelves behind him.

"They were real there, you see—that's why I took them with me, in my innocence. But they changed as soon as I passed through the door. Here they are different, just shadows of themselves." He sighed and added, "Like my life, since then."

Because the queen had never called him back.

He hadn't known why either. He hadn't known about the Hunter until now, which was why he was so happy when I told him. He hadn't even known what was special about the horn he was holding—had thought it was just any old Stranger object. And he hadn't been able to figure out why the few weeks had stretched out so long. He'd been waiting for hundreds and hundreds of years.

While he waited, he tried to tell people about the Strangers. No one would believe him. Finally he had to accept the fact that most people thought his stories were just imaginary tales and silly superstitions. He became a folklore expert, and he traveled all over England telling people the truth and letting them believe it was just lies.

But everywhere he went, after a while, things began to happen—wicked things, awful things. He'd know it was because of that door that had been left open for him, and that he'd have to move on to somewhere new.

But the door always moved with him. And the Strangers always came through it.

Finally he couldn't take it anymore. He couldn't bear the responsibility. He decided to get far away from any place where Strangers had ever been seen or even been believed in. He thought if he came far away from England to a place like Winnipeg, the door wouldn't be able to follow him.

He was wrong. It took longer, but it came here, too.

The first thing that made him realize it was hearing about Liam. A Stranger had come here, had somehow wandered here by accident. Through a door. He'd taken Liam in because he felt responsible for him.

Well, it was nice to hear he felt something for Liam, even if it was just feeling responsible. And he didn't even have to feel that anymore, did he? Was it his stay in Stranger country that had made Mr. Rhymer so cold? Poor Liam. Maybe he was better off as a Yelper.

Anyway, once Liam appeared, Rhymer knew the door was nearby again. But he didn't do anything about it. He was old, and he was tired. He just hoped the Strangers would go away. He tried to ignore the signs, until it was too late. Until the Changeling came and the Yelpers and all the rest. Until I got involved and had to make my journey.

So it really was his fault, just like he said. Because of him, my sister had been stolen away. Because of him, I'd lost my allowance and my body, I'd been attacked by Yelpers and insulted by piles of turds and mugged by a girl with green teeth. Because of him, Liam had wandered out of his own world and lost everything. And all the time we were all just minor sideshows, random accidents. It was really Mr. Rhymer who was the main event.

He was such a harmless-looking old man. No one looking at him would ever guess he could have caused so much trouble.

And talk about things seeming different than they appeared. For all those centuries when he didn't know about the Hunter, he'd just thought the queen didn't want him anymore. Now he knew different. Now the message had come, the message he and the queen had agreed on—and it had turned out to be the Hunter's horn—a horn to blow him home. Now the way was clear, and he could return to her.

"Which I will do, right now," he said. "There's nothing else for me to do here, and I can wait no longer. Please lock the door behind you as you leave. You just push in the button in the knob."

And before I could say or do anything, he put the horn up to his lips and blew.

I tried to stop him, afraid that the hounds would come, the Yelpers.

But Mr. Rhymer knew what he was doing. The Hunter was gone, and no hounds came, not this time. The loud, clear notes he was blowing suddenly cut off. In a flash, Mr. Rhymer was gone.

Gone. Blown home. Andrea and I were alone in his office, alone with all those paper swords and paper crowns.

And one new paper object. Right in the middle of the desk, in front of where Mr. Rhymer had just been sitting, was a paper horn.

Twenty-two

Somehow, being in the same room with that paper horn gave me the creeps. I got out of there as fast as I could, locking the door behind me as requested, and Andrea and I waited for the cabbie out in the hallway.

After a blissfully uneventful cab trip with a driver who looked nothing like a Walt Disney dwarf and who was too bored to even notice my bathrobe or jeer at my mocs, we pulled up in front of the house on Wavell. Home at last. I gave the cabbie the twenty, hustled Andrea around the back, opened the door as quietly as I could, and snuck into the kitchen. I hoped nobody would be there. I didn't want my parents seeing Andrea as long as they thought the other Andrea was the real one.

Dad was sitting at the kitchen table, hidden behind the newspaper. I put my hand over Andrea's mouth to keep her quiet, which did not make her happy. She squirmed a lot.

"Is that you, John?" Dad said, not even looking up. "Where have you been, out so early on a Saturday morning?"

I didn't answer. He didn't really care, and I was concentrating on trying to sneak Andrea past him without dropping her. She was squirming so much she knocked my hand off her mouth, and she let out a yelp.

"Good," he said, not even realizing the noise was her and not me.

By then we'd reached the hallway.

"Don't bother your mom, John," Dad said, still not looking up from the paper. "She's lying down. Had some kind of scare or something. Seems to be imagining things. Too many Stephen King movies, if you ask me. Humph."

Lying down, eh? Sounded perfect. I went upstairs, and then I slowly inched open the door of my parents' bedroom.

My mom seemed to be asleep, and the fake Andrea was lying there snoring on the bed beside her. I can't tell you how mad it made me, seeing that disgusting creature lying there all hairy and wrinkled like that on my parents' bed, and my mom thinking it was just a baby. Her baby.

I put the real Andrea down on the floor, said

"Shush" to her, and crept toward the bed as quietly as I could. Then I took the little jar the queen had given me out of my bathrobe pocket, opened it, and quickly, before Mom could move or anything, dabbed some of the gooey stuff on her eyelids.

She flinched and then began to rub her eyes—rubbing the stuff in more, I was glad to see. And then she opened her eyes and looked at me.

"John," she said. "What are you doing in here? Why are you—?" She gazed in a bewildered way all around the room. And then her gaze hit on the thing lying beside her.

She shrieked. Shrieked and stared. She seemed to be immobilized—so shocked she couldn't think of what to do or say.

The shriek woke up the Changeling. His eyes blinked open, and he saw her staring at him with that look of horror. And he knew he'd been discovered.

And before I even realized it had happened, he had gone. There was nobody lying on the bed. The minute he knew Mom could see him for himself, he was out of there. He was probably already back home—back with the queen and Mr. Rhymer, in the country of the Strangers.

Good riddance to very bad rubbish.

Mom blinked, totally confused. Had she seen something or hadn't she? She obviously didn't know.

"I could swear the baby was there," she said, "and then . . ."

She turned toward me as she spoke, and suddenly she was seeing something else she had not expected to see.

It was Andrea. The real Andrea. By this time she'd crawled over to the bed and had managed to lift herself up so that her head was popping up over the edge of the bed.

Mom gasped. She stared at Andrea. Andrea stared back. Then she smiled and opened her mouth.

"Momma!" she said.

After that it was sheer bedlam. Mom leaped toward Andrea and picked her up and hugged her, all the time screaming stuff about how her baby was okay again, it was a miracle, and like that. All this noise was too much even for Dad, who finally put down his paper and came to investigate, and then he got even more excited than Mom.

The rest of that day is just a blur. There were phone calls to doctors, there were relatives and friends coming over. Everyone was amazed about the change in Andrea, and nobody could account for it.

Me, I said nothing, just stayed in the background and smiled a lot. I had my sister back. I had my mom and my dad back. I had my family back again.

Mr. Rhymer's disappearance was in the news, of course. But they just suggested that he had amnesia or something, and had wandered off.

Liam didn't even make it into the news. In

fact, nobody even seems to notice that he isn't around anymore, not even at school. Poor Liam. It's as if he'd never been here in our world, never existed at all.

Sometimes, you know, I wonder if he did exist, if any of it really did happen, or if I just imagined it all.

But then I suddenly notice that the fork or pencil or piece of toilet paper I'm holding is in my left hand.

And every once in a while, I get chased out of a store or yelled at by a total stranger on the street, and I realize once more how busy that Cowalker was. And I know it was real, all right.

But it's over now, blissfully over, and things are pretty well back to normal. No stray dogs barking in the night. No hollow people in Safeway. My folks are fine, too. The silence and the yelling are a thing of the past, and Andrea zooms all over the place and gets into everything and drives us all crazy.

We love every minute of it.

Someday, I hope, even Rob and Mark will stop being pissed off at me for ruining the big night they were planning with those so-called babes at the community club, and start talking to me again. Just a few words would do.

They could even be words about body-checking.

A Historical Note

The Strangers are a conservative folk, and they stick to their old habits. Much of what this book reports of recent events in the Riverview district of Winnipeg is similar to earlier records of Stranger activities centuries ago, in various parts of the British Isles.

The Sky Yelpers, the Cowalker, and Jenny Greenteeth all once did their tricks there. Groups of mounted Strangers rode together in what was called the Fairy Rade, and it was such a Rade that carried Johnny to the castle of the Strangers. Other Strangers were known to have squeezed the blood out of humans while they danced with them. And the Hunter's body originally belonged to the great hero Cuchulain, who really was something, just as Johnny suspected.

In those days, Changelings frequently replaced human babies, and even more frequently were suspected to have done so, with the horrific results Liam described.

Humans also frequently found themselves in Stranger country, and ate the food there at their peril. One such human was an earlier Kathleen Fordyce; and an earlier Johnny Nesbit once happened to see her through the side of a hill. No one knows what he did about it, or if he ever saw her again.

Mr. Rhymer's romance with the queen was first described in the fourteenth-century poem "The Ballad of Thomas the Rhymer." I think Mr. Rhymer might have written the poem himself, after he first returned from Stranger country. Oral tradition has long prophesied that he would be recalled to that country in his old age.

The most complete and accurate reports of Strangers and their habits can be found in a wonderful book by Katharine Briggs: *A Dictionary of Fairies, Brownies, Bogies, and Other Supernatural Creatures* (Penguin).